TUNNELS INTO TIME

They appeared on the horizon, twin pillars of black tornado funnels over 100,000 feet high.

From his hiding place, wedged between three large boulders, Rockson shielded his face against the stinging wind and witnessed an awesome phenomenon.

The sands of the Utah desert, billions upon billions of tons, were rushing into the eye of the storm—a spectacle on a universal scale of Nature gone mad. The air was filled with lightning. And then, in the flash of an instant, a massive vacuum formed and collapsed. Desert and polar winds collided and the dynamic forces converted into a massive implosion-explosion.

And Rockson felt himself being sucked up from his hiding place into the wild blue yonder . . .

#10 AMERICAN NIGHTMARE

BY RYDER STACY

ZEBRA BOOKS
KENSINGTON PUBLISHING CORP.

ZEBRA BOOKS

are published by

Kensington Publishing Corp.
475 Park Avenue South
New York, NY 10016

First printing: March 1987

Printed in the United States of America

Chapter 1

The vulture soared high above the slowly moving dot that its keen eyes tracked far below. It waited, circling endlessly, moving forward every so often to keep directly above the figure on the broiling sands of the desert. For three days the vulture had watched this solitary creature stagger across the sands below. The figure was moving more slowly now; the vulture sensed it was near its end. The bird of prey flew closer to the ground, knowing its long wait was nearly over. Soon the two-legged creature would stop forever — the vulture's keen dark eyes shone with something approaching anticipation. Its beak opened slightly. Soon . . . soon it would eat.

The dark bird flashed before the white-hot face of the sun, sending down a bit of shade. The solitary man stopped and looked up at the sky. He grimaced. The vulture, his companion, his *funeral director*, was still with him — only closer.

"Not yet, old friend, not yet . . ." said the man. For three days now, Ted Rockson had trekked the

Utah desert. He was tired and thirsty. And though the tawny-skinned mutant warrior of twenty-first-century Free America was a special man whose physique had been shaped by mutated genes that inured him to great hardship, he was near his end. His genetic inheritance made him stronger than any man of the last century . . . but still a man needed water and food.

On he walked, not daring to stop for an instant. His bleeding kneecap poked through his torn pants. It still hurt — as did his wrenched shoulder — from the ordeal he'd been through: the mission to the far north. He had managed to set down his stolen Soviet jet in a canyon, only to see it crushed by falling rocks. Then he had begun the long walk, with a small gourd filled with stream water — long ago consumed.

He had to hang on. Had to get across the broiling wastelands to his hidden underground home base — Century City — headquarters of the Freefighters of America. He must live, fight on with all his might. For even now, over a hundred years after the surprise Soviet nuke attack that had devastated America, the battle raged: freedom versus totalitarianism. Ted Rockson, a.k.a. the Doomsday Warrior, still battled to wrest liberty from the Soviet occupiers. As *the* symbol of American resistance, his death would be a blow to freedom.

God, he was hot in his sealskin parka. But he dared not remove it. It was his only protection from the white-hot sun that beat down unmercifully, threatening to bake him alive. Besides, at night the temperature in this desolate area dropped to twenty degrees below. Not that he'd see another night. It seemed pointless, but nevertheless he'd go on.

He placed one foot in front of the other, vowing that he'd not give up. The vulture would have to wait some more . . . But twenty minutes later, he fell to his knees. He looked around one more time. And in his burning, painful, nearly blinded eyes he spotted something: a long sinewy green rope winding down from a sandy hillock. What the hell?

Unable to stand, he crawled closer, on hands and knees. He was about to touch it when he realized what it was — vegetable matter, living vegetable matter. A root of some kind that might secure a plant to the shifting sands. It could be dangerous to touch it, if it belonged to the plant he suspected lay at its end.

He crawled on, after a minute reaching the top of the sandy hill, and saw that at its very summit, sitting like a sentinel in the heat-rippling day, was a squat, cabbage-like plant of the desert — the bloodfruit plant. It was a very special plant. The bloodfruit's juicy fruit, at the core of the odd spiky plant's curled leaves, was bitter but nutritious. A godsend to a desperate desert traveler. He scrambled up the sand dune to reach it.

He was elated, for here was both food and water. He eagerly approached the plant — and was relieved to see that no scavenger of the desert had come before him and shorn it of its prize — its single bulbous central fruit. He was careful not to disturb the bloodfruit plant's long tendrils which splayed out like spider's legs on the sands. Rockson knew they would twist around an unwary animal's body and entrap it. Then they would bring the eater into the plant's mouthlike organ, hidden in the sand — and devour it

7

with acid juices. The plant was carnivorous. It could even kill a man who was weak after days of desert wandering. Knowing this, he leaned carefully over the plant's starlike core, and taking his knife out of his belt, he cut the red, ripe fruit out of the plant's center. When he'd scrambled a sufficient distance from the feeler-tendrils, he stuck his knife into the fruit so that he could drink of its essence.

Ah, it was so good, so fresh and juicy, and not even bitter. A good pint of sap. Filled with pulp.

Rockson relaxed a bit. Things were looking up. He even sprinkled a few drops of his fevered brow.

He ate of the thick pulp, cutting the remainder into narrow strips that he tied to his belt for eating later.

Refreshed, he walked onward. The sky began to cloud over; the temperature dropped to a tolerable level. The earth's atmosphere, thinned by the nuke holocaust of a century earlier, let in more sunrays in the daytime. Cloud cover moderated that; and cloud cover tonight meant he could expect temperatures in this desolate area of Utah to drop to just below freezing. Too cold for an average man, but he was a hardy mutant. The white streak down the center of his black mane of hair, his lack of beard, his keen but mismatched dark blue and aquamarine eyes, attested to that. Given a chance, he'd survive the trek now, he'd make it.

But something happened. Just when it all seemed possible again, just when he was sure he'd make it — a pain rose in his gut. Then another pain that nearly doubled over the brave Freefighter the Soviet enemy called the Ultimate American.

His strength was no match for the poison — he

8

realized that's what it was. The bloodfruit must have been a different species from those near Century City. It had some sort of toxin in it. Shoving his fingers into his throat he tried to puke it up, but to no avail. The poison had been absorbed by his moisture-starved body.

Retching, he collapsed on the sands. Soon, weird images danced in his fevered brain. He lay in a fetal position through the freezing night—hours of torture, then dawn.

He felt slightly better as the temperature rose abruptly. Perhaps, he thought, the worst might be over—perhaps he'd ingested a nonfatal dose. He was feeling odd, but much better. He got up, started off again. He felt a cool shift in the air; a change in the weather was coming. His burning eyes searched the sky.

There. Due east—a darkness sweeping over the desert. A cloud, some sort of storm. It could be a dust storm, or only rain. If it *was* rain, it might be brief. The desert would soak it up; he'd be left only with what he could gather in his hands. And he'd soon be thirsty again. Man needs a pint of water a day. If he could put his parched lips below a runoff, or find a hole that collected water in a rock outcropping, he'd drink to his content.

If it was a dust storm coming, he'd most likely die. The granular particles, moving at a hundred miles per hour, would do him in. Dust storms out this way lasted for days.

He saw flashes of distant lightning—that didn't tell the story one way or the other. Lightning was a part of both types of storm.

He moved onward, looking for a boulder, an outcropping, *anything* that might hold precious water if and when the rains came. The rolling clouds cast phantasmagoric shadows on the sands.

And before him suddenly he saw not a pile of rocks but a verdant oasis, palms waving in the cool breeze. The scene wavered slightly in a heat ripple. It was beautiful, serene.

How far? It was hard to tell—it could be a hundred yards or less. With an exclamation of joy, he ran toward it.

In a hundred feet, he knew the dreadful truth. The oasis evaporated. A *mirage*. Damned mirage.

He laughed. He fell down on his knees, laughing. The first drops of rain from the sodden sky hit him in that position.

Water. Rock opened his mouth, took in a few precious drops. *Quick*, he told himself take off your shirt, make a bowl of bunched material. It will soak up some, but *maybe*, if the rain is hard enough . . .

The ground grew darker, absorbing the big drops that now fell. His laughter at his folly turned to joy; peals of joy. The cupped fabric of his shirt started filling with water. The sky was dark now, the lightning brilliant, terrifying peals of thunder ripping at his ears. The wind was whipping up.

He drank, rubbed the wet shirt over his sunburnt face, cupped the material again, filled it, drank again. He was feeling better. He looked up. The line squall was already passing, but there was a strange, distant roar—constant, low, *but there*. A huge storm was brewing. High winds and mega-lightning. But for now the rain let up. His vision was better, his heart beat more regularly. You could now see for a dozen miles—and Rockson, sweeping the far horizon with his gaze, detected a plateau glinting like gold below an arching rainbow. It was over a thousand feet high if an inch. And it was unmistakable. The Glower's Plateau! He had passed this way years ago, while on a mission to secure a new super-weapon for the Freefighters. The mica-filled plateau was an unmistakable landmark. He knew his way now, for sure. He'd try to live on just the water he had imbibed, if he could. Another day, maybe two, of hard trekking and he'd see *his* mountains. He'd be home at long last. He watched the sun setting behind the plateau. Let's see, he knew that the sun set in the southwest this time of year in North America, and if his memory didn't deceive him, the plateau was near the old site of Salt Lake City, which had been blasted to dust in the nuke war. To reach Colorado, he'd head off at a ninety-degree angle to the left of the plateau.

If he could just avoid hypothermia—extreme loss of body heat—tonight . . . Perhaps he would have to cover himself with the red dirt he now trod over. That would keep some heat in—a dirt sleeping bag.

There was a noise—mechanical—a vehicle. Rockson dropped to the ground, flat. Shit! It was a jeep! Over to the west. He hadn't seen it, because it was coming out of the glare of the setting sun.

Voices—Russian words. *Reds.* A patrol. They were only a few hundred yards away. Had they spotted him?

He was unarmed, except for the knife. If they *had* spotted him, he was probably a goner.

A tall Soviet officer with a gold left eyetooth

11

glinting in the sunlight stood laughing and pointing in the lead jeep. Pointing at Rockson. He was saying something about "follow the poor bastard, until he drops, but do it slowly. . . ." He was saying something about taking bets on how long the solitary man would last—Rock knew enough Russian to understand that much.

Maybe, the Doomsday Warrior thought, just *maybe* I can smash that gold eyetooth down his foul-breathed gullet. Maybe I'll see if he laughs then.

It was a tall order, for the jeep contained six men, all armed with Kalashnikov submachine guns. And there was another jeep coming up behind it.

Chapter 2

Lieutenant Lev Streltsy of the Soviet KGB was an ambitious and clever young officer. The descendant of an ancient Russian family whose ancestors had enjoyed privilege and favor from the tsars, Streltsy considered himself a rising star, anxious for opportunity. Little did he expect that the strange fugitive his squad had spotted and were now pursuing could be just that opportunity.

Most of the men stationed at the remote Petroff Fortress in the Utah desert considered their assignment odious. Not Streltsy. Proud and opportunistic, he found the nearly forgotten post ideally suited to his long-range secret dream: to lead a coup against the Soviet hierarchy in the West and establish himself as a modern-day star with North America as his personal domain and kingdom. Fort Petroff would serve ideally as his base of operations. Not only was it isolated beyond the watchful eyes of powerful administrators, but the garrison force of 1200 KGB operatives and young trainees provided a ready collection of misfits and nonconformists from which he could mold a cadre of loyal personal guards to support his

13

counterrevolution. Since the leader of the KGB, Killov, had fallen from power, this had begun to be more than a mere dream.

The officers' corps at Petroff also suited Streltsy. Comprised primarily of aged, unimaginative senior officers, Streltsy had quickly consolidated his position. The base commandant, Lieutenant General Fydor Dommsky, was more than willing to let the able young KGB officer assume the burden of command at his frontier post while he idled away the days with strong drink and sleep.

Streltsy had won the affection and loyalty of the garrison by appeasing their meaner instincts. He had regular shipments of vodka and other luxuries dropped at the base by cohorts in the Soviet Air Force. These he distributed freely to the men and they soon formed a jolly company of swashbuckling musketeers, devoted to their leader. Growing irreverent and bold in their isolation, the men openly mocked the military establishment that had banished them to this remote and desolate duty. On more than one occasion, during their drunken revelries, Streltsy had hinted at his grand schemes, and found his men receptive to the idea of rebellion.

To further activate their taste for blood and avarice, Streltsy had built a secret torture chamber. The "Bastille," as the men called their playground, was a remarkable collection of medieval and modern torture devices that would have made Ivan the Terrible envious. Located deep underground in an abandoned missile silo several miles from the base, the Bastille served as a secret headquarters and pleasure palace for Streltsy's band. Unwary travelers picked up by his men in their foraging patrols usually ended up screaming in agony in the Bastille. Many of the prisoners were kept alive as servants to the marauding KGB squads. Streltsy made sure his men were provided with mistresses and slaves to wet their appetites for the new order he envisioned.

To Rockson, a Russian was a Russian: scheming, clever, disgruntled, ambitious, or whatever . . . they were all poison to him. And, despite his fatigue and nausea, he intended to do his best to avoid joining the "jolly company" of KGB'ers coming after him. He knew from the uniforms that these were Killov's sickboys and he was sure that their welcoming committee had more than tea planned for him when he finally gave out.

In any case, the game was on — Rockson now walking slowly through the maze of sand dunes and boulder fields that dotted the broad desert plain, while the Soviet jeeps tailed him from a distance, taunting him. Under normal circumstances, that much negligence on the part of the enemy would have been more than enough of an advantage for Rockson to secure his escape, or even destroy them. But the bloodfruit he had eaten was affecting his mind as well as his body. He was fighting to maintain control. But the nausea and fatigue, coupled with the burning desert sun and dehydration, were taking their toll. His eyes burned and his temples pounded with pain. The weight of his arms pulled them down limply as he shuffled along barely able to grasp the knife in his right hand, his only weapon.

He searched the landscape for a break in the terrain, a place to hide just for a minute, enough to pull his heaving stomach together and rest his aching legs. There . . . just ahead . . . about fifty yards. A narrow defile thick with leafy undergrowth . . . perhaps an escape hatch. He renewed his effort, expending his final reserve of energy, his mind racing with anticipation. Bullets were suddenly unleashed, short bursts from automatic rifles kicking up sand around his feet. They were missing on purpose. If only he could make the defile. Closer and closer . . . another ten steps. He dove for the cover, landing in a belly flop on a stretch of salt flat, the lush green foliage disappearing as the wisp of mirage it was. Rock spat a mouthful of briny sand.

"Looks like I'm about ready for a Section Eight," Rock muttered, referring to the military regulation regarding discharge for psychological instability.

The jeeps were no more than fifty yards off now and Rock could hear the Russians laughing and jeering at him.

"Running dog," they laughed, peppering the ground around him with bursts of fire. He tried to stand, flopped back.

Within seconds they came screaming by, firing their weapons inches from him as he crawled and stumbled, the jeeps' fat tires inches away. They began circling the distressed Freefighter, laughing and screaming like cowboys of old.

Rock spun on the verge of panic and delirium. He couldn't believe it would end like this. Knocked off by a band of KGB renegades in the desert, his body left to bake in the sun while scorpions scurried through his rotted cranium. In a final surge of effort he spun with a scream and heaved a rock he picked up at the windshield of one of the circling jeeps. He saw the glass shatter and the jeep spin out of control, then a fierce thud cracked his skull from behind and he was out.

Rockson awoke to find himself in a windowless, circular room. Metal walls laced with catwalks rose some sixty feet upward. He was strapped on his back to what appeared to be a large metal spoked wheel, his arms and legs stretched tight and secured with metal shackles. All around the spacious enclosure he could discern a variety of strange contraptions, vaguely familiar but unrecognizable. He shook his head to clear his vision and struggled weakly against his bindings.

Peering upward into the huge cylinder, his senses began to return.

"A silo," he whispered, "a missile silo."

"Correct, my friend," replied a voice from above and behind him. "Emptied of its contents in the nuke war one hundred and three years ago."

Rock craned his neck but could not see his adversary. Suddenly the wheel spun halfway around with a sound of electric gears, and Rock could see the man who had spoken. It was the man from the lead jeep, seated before a control panel on a platform about fifteen feet up on the wall. Five or six of his cronies clustered around him, and footsteps on the myriad of metal walkways up and down the silo told him there were others.

"Welcome to the Bastille. Formerly a missile silo, used to house one of the A-bombs your forefathers dispensed on my country in the great war. A house of death, if you will." The gold-toothed man smiled an evil grin. "A temple of the devil, is it not?"

"What . . . what do you want from me? . . ." Rock gasped, feigning fear. In tight situations, making the opponent underestimate you is a useful strategy. In truth Rockson was not afraid.

The charade brought a hideous laugh from the Soviet lieutenant. He set the control to a slow spin and descended the stairway to the silo floor.

"Why, I'm surprised at you. An esteemed Freefighter such as you styling yourself quaking in fear at the sight of a mere lieutenant."

"Freefighter?" Rock replied, continuing the ruse. The wheel was spinning slowly, causing Rock to twist his head back and forth as he watched the officer approach. He and his henchmen began countercircling the spinning wheel.

"Freefighter. yes. Come now, Mr. Rockson, Mr. Ted Rockson, self-styled leader of the American Resistance movement. Surely you haven't contracted amnesia along with your other predicaments?"

"Rockson? Please. . . . I don't know what you're talking about. My name's Alvin. Alvin York. I'm a prospector. I don't mean no harm. What do you want from me?"

Streltsy stopped the wheel with his hand and came face to face with his prisoner.

"Don't play games with me, Rockson," he said low, deadly serious. "We get news dispatches even here. Any Soviet officer worth his salt has seen your picture a hundred times. I must say, Mr. Rockson, I'm grateful you chose to stumble into my web."

"And who are you?" asked Rockson.

"Streltsy. Lieutenant Lev Streltsy, KGB. Remember the name. If you are fortunate enough to survive your impending ordeals," he said, waving to the collection of contraptions around the room, "you will undoubtedly hear much of me."

"I'll ask you again, Lieutenant," said Rock, "what do you want?"

"Answers, my friend. Answers," replied Streltsy, releasing the wheel and continuing his strut, his tall gaunt countenance passing Rock's field of vision every five seconds or so. Rock saw he had the traditional dueling scar crossing the length of his left cheek, lending an ominous aura to the man's gaunt face, his insolent sneer.

"Your friends, your plans, your weapons, supplies. I am a profoundly curious man, Mr. Rockson, and I believe there is much you can tell me. Providence has placed you in my hands. It is another indication of my destiny. You can provide me with enough information to ferret out and virtually eliminate the core of resistance in America. *You*, my dear friend, are just the opportunity I have been hoping for. You see, Mr. Rockson, besides being a curious man, I am an ambitious man. I see great things in my future. Like you, I am not altogether satisfied with the power structure of the world in its present state. In a sense, we are allies, Mr. Rockson. You are fortunate in that respect. A lesser man would have quickly turned you over to his superiors where your fate would have been sealed. The Premier himself would be most anxious to interview you. Have you ever seen Red Square, my friend?"

"No," said Rockson, immediately regretting the lie. He knew he was in a psychological game, one that was almost sure to end in his death. Answering any question was a dangerous precedent.

"Ahh, very good. Very good. And there is no need for you to make this trip. We are similar men, Rockson. I am well aware of your prowess and abilities. Perhaps I might even have a place for you on my staff."

"Great," said Rockson. "Do I get an office with a window and a key to the Kremlin's men's room?"

Streltsy chuckled and switched the wheel to a stop, ending Rock's dizzying spin.

"Enough idle chitchat, my friend. Now, on to business. Where were you heading when we picked you up? Who were you planing to rendezvous with?"

"I was on my way to Capistrano to meet up with a regiment of swallows in search of worms, not unlike yourself."

Again the lieutenant chuckled, and again the wheel began a slow spin. Streltsy picked up a thick leather strap and slapped it against the palm of his hand.

"This device is called a knout," Streltsy said. "It was a favorite device of the ancient tsars. They found it most useful in extracting confessions. Look about you, Mr. Rockson. I am most proud of my collection of torture devices, most constructed with my own hands from designs that have been in my family for generations. Now, we can avoid mutilating your sound body if you cooperate. These devices reach beyond the realm of pain, Mr. Rockson. I assure you,

20

you will not be harmed *if* you talk. I have told you I am your friend. A kindred spirit. You can rest assured you'll be given a chance to join my growing revolutionary army. Together, we will throw off the yoke of oppression and establish a new state based on the ancient principles."

"A fine speech, your lordship," Rock mocked. "Now, shall we get on with the torture and get it over with? I'm growing weary of your lectures."

Streltsy landed a blow across Rockson's chest, cutting through his sealskin vest and leaving a painful welt across his body. "I will release you from the wheel for now. Perhaps a few hours with Comrade Relsk, the Bear, will make you cooperate," Streltsy said. "We shall talk again soon." He muttered something in Russian to his men, then left, pattering quickly up the steel staircase to the catwalk.

Rockson heard a metal door creak open, and turned his head to see a bare-chested, smoothly bald figure the size of a sumo wrestler waddle out of an adjoining room. The man smiled a toothless grin, approached with heavy, ponderous barefooted steps.

To say the least, things didn't look good.

They *weren't*. He was beaten senseless by a bearlike Relsk. The monstrously beefy torture-chamber attendant knew what he was doing, having done it so often. Rock was pummeled until he showed signs of passing out. He was doused then, with cold water, and injected with chemical stimulants to keep him awake. But Rockson's mind-training kept him partially numb.

When Streltsy returned he found Rockson hanging from two fingers while the big Soviet worked the

21

vicious knout across his back. His legs had been tied ankle to ankle then chained to a ring in the floor. He hung from his two index fingers, his feet six inches off the ground, swaying to the rhythmic lashings of the heavy leather. Relsk worked up and down his back, each blow falling just below the other, leaving a trail of welts.

"Cut him loose," said Streltsy as he descended the stairway.

His man obeyed, cutting Rockson's finger bindings. When he fell down, they put him on a wooden chair while Streltsy marched to a small table and began preparing two syringes.

"Revive him," he said.

They doused him with icy water and pulled his head back by the hair, slapping his face viciously. The Doomsday Warrior groaned.

"Now," said Streltsy, advancing toward Rockson. "We shall see what our friend had learned in the past few hours."

"He's a tough one," said one of the men. "Not a whimper from him."

"Perhaps this pentothal will help," Streltsy said, shooting a heavy dose of the truth serum into Rockson's arm. He was placed on a cot. Rock, barely conscious, was dimly aware of the proceedings. He had undergone torture before, even truth-serum injections. Mustering his iron will, he knew he'd have the strength to resist. He wouldn't give away Century City's location.

Streltsy gave the drug a few minutes to take effect, then added a healthy dose of adrenaline to Rock's bloodstream to bring him fully around.

Rock felt the surge of energy shoot through his system and raised his head.

"Let's talk," said Streltsy calmly, pulling a chair up in front of the Freefighter. "Are you in pain?"

"Yes and no," said Rockson, fighting the effects of the drugs. "We know how to block pain, make it feel like tickles."

"Tell me about yourself," Streltsy continued. "You must have led a fascinating life. Where is your base, this fabled Century City?"

"I used to dream about cowboys," Rockson said, unable to keep from talking, but trying to dwell on irrelevent topics.

"Ahh, cowboys," said Streltsy, grabbing the string. "The old American West. Yes yes. A fascinating period. Tell me, what fascinated you about cowboys?"

"Rugged. Tough. Men who rode the open range and slept under the stars. The country must have been . . . so beautiful . . ."

"Yes yes. True," replied Streltsy. "But their lives were not always pleasant. They lived in an untamed land, with no law. Not like Colorado."

"Yes," said Rockson. He sensed the flow of the conversation.

"Century City is in New Mexico, where the Grand Canyon makes a right turn into Arizona," Rock lied. "The Indians lived there once."

Streltsy's face turned red. *"You lie,"* he snarled. "We know that Century City is in Colorado somewhere. We know that much. So this gentle method doesn't work on you, does it, Rockson? Well, then, there is only the wheel. We will strap you to the wheel

23

and watch you spin until blood spurts from your eyes, your nose, your mouth. But maybe before you die, you will tell us what we need to know. Take him to the wheel!"

The soldiers did as Streltsy ordered. Soon Rockson again was face-up in the middle of the circular room, strapped hands and feet to "the wheel." The wheel was just that: a huge metal wheel with flat spokes wide enough to place a body on. Rockson's body. Since the wheel had a twelve-foot diameter, it was possible to place Rockson's feet at the center of the wheel, and his head at the wheel's edge.

When he was trussed up so that he couldn't move an inch, Streltsy came over to him and leered down at him. "Perhaps you understand the pain you will soon endure. I ask you one more time—where is Century City?"

Rockson gathered some spittle and ejected it straight in the Russian's face. "Go to hell, you bastard."

Streltsy punched him in the face and snapped out the order to let the wheel begin turning.

As the wheel began to turn, Rockson saw a table at the far end of the room—a card table, one of those snap-open kind. And on the table was a chessboard and pieces. The chessmen were all lined up on their original squares. No game was in progress. The Russians were zealots for chess.

"Wait," Rockson called out. "Streltsy, I have a proposition for you—better than seeing blood spurt out of my ears. You know," he said as the room spun around faster and faster, "I will never reveal Century City's location by means like this. But stop the wheel.

I'll play a chess game with you—if you win, I'll talk!"

For a dreadful half minute the wheel continued accelerating. Rockson felt the blood collecting in his head, his legs going numb. If this kept up, he'd burst a blood vessel any second . . .

Suddenly Streltsy shouted, "Stop the wheel! I want to play this man."

Rockson was unstrapped and escorted to the chessboard. He could hardly walk, his legs were so numb; and his head was still reeling from the wheel. Streltsy sat down opposite him. "Let's get this straight. If I win, you give me your word of honor—I'm aware it's good—that you will tell me what I want to know?"

Rockson paused, waiting for the room to stop spinning. "Yes," said Rockson, "and if I win—I go free." Rockson was careful not to mention that he was the Inter-Free City chess champion.

Streltsy's eyes lit up, going for the deal. "I'm the number two ranked grandmaster of the Western Hemisphere. I will polish you off in minutes. It's a deal. I accept your offer. I give you my word as an officer."

Rockson nodded. "Good. Let's play."

Rockson had counted on his fantastic memory of past chess games he had studied to carry him through. But Streltsy, if he was a grandmaster, would know those games too. Still, there was nothing to do but go on with the game.

Streltsy said he wanted red, Rockson would play white. They sat down at the table and Rockson said, "First, could I have a little water?"

Streltsy laughed. "After we play."

With all the guns pointed at him, Rockson had no

choice but to play by Streltsy's rules. *No water* being one of them. The Soviet generously—no, overconfidently—let Rock make first move, which Rockson knew gave a slight advantage.

The game began, the soldiers huddled in a circle around the board, cheering on their leader.

Rockson didn't play his best game by far, but Streltsy was worse!

ROCKSON	STRELTSY
1. P–K4	P–QB4
2. N–KB3	N–QB3
3. P–Q4	PxP
4. NxP	P–K4
5. N–B5	KN–K2
6. N–Q6 Mate!	

Rockson had defeated the Soviet grandmaster in a mere six moves!

"Impossible," gasped the Soviet lieutenant.

"Obviously it *isn't* impossible, Streltsy. Now I want my glass of water, and then I want to be freed, as you promised."

Streltsy smiled. "I say you cheated. You *forfeit* the game! But you will get your wish to be outside. I think I would like to see you dragged behind my jeep for a few miles. The apt punishment for cheating."

Rockson had had only faint hope that the Soviet would keep his word. Streltsy had given it freely only because he was convinced he couldn't lose. But now, to cover up his fallibility to his men, or just because he was a bastard—it didn't matter—he was going back on his word.

They tied Rockson's hands together and led him up the spiral stairs to the surface. He had to hop because they tied his ankles too.

Once up on the desert, Streltsy jumped up into the back of a jeep. "Ivan, attach a rope to Mr. Rockson's hands. Tie the other end to the rear bumper of the jeep."

There were a half-dozen Kalashnikovs trained on Rockson. Now, unfortunately, was not the time to make a move. They started to drag him.

Rockson twisted and spat as the gathering desert winds kicked up a powerful blast of sand, almost blinding him.

"It looks like a storm building up," one of the Russian soldiers said to Streltsy. "Perhaps we should head back to the silo."

"Nyet," Streltsy barked. "This is my pigeon. I won't turn over a prize like Rockson to that sloth General Dommsky. Why let him get credit for the capture? Don't you see what we have here, you fool? If he collaborates with us, we can use the information to our own benefit. If he is foolish enough to resist, I personally will turn his body over to Premier Vassily. Start the engine."

The jeep thrust forward with Streltsy standing in the rear and Rockson skidding painfully over the rugged desert floor. Rockson was in a near-delirious state. He had never fully recovered from the effects of the poison fruit he had eaten, and the succession of torture and drugs his body had endured had only increased his distance from reality.

But it was cooler, much cooler. The *storm*!

He saw a glimmer of hope in the burgeoning storm that was beginning to encompass the entire horizon. The wind was growing fiercer by the minute, reducing visibility and improving his chance for escape—if he could loosen the rope.

The jeep moved slowly at first and Rockson managed to position his body so that the ropes on his wrists scraped the surface, wearing the fibers thin and allowing him to hope he could break them.

He bounced painfully across the sand as the jeep detoured through beds of cactus and rocky outcroppings wherever they appeared. Rockson twisted and writhed in pain, but could see that the Russians were becoming preoccupied with the gathering storm. He pulled himself up to where the rope attached to his wrists and began gnawing at it, sliding along on his side.

Streltsy, standing in the back of the jeep, could barely see his victim through the sandstorm. Rockson, dragging some sixty feet away, had successfully reversed himself and grasped onto the rope with his hands. He tugged frantically at the fraying fibers, pushing fist against mighty fist.

The storm was cooperating divinely now, providing an effective screen between Rockson and his tormentors. As the jeep struck out along a rocky road leading up an incline, Rock searched through the blinding, whirling sands. Visibility was no more than twenty or thirty feet, and he figured they would soon stop. Then he saw what he was looking for: a large boulder along the side of the road. Nearing it, the jeep made a swerving turn. Rockson, with his last strength, snapped the rope at the worn knot between his hands. He was free.

His body rolled with the force of his momentum, tumbling over the edge of the road and down the steep incline.

The jeep disappeared up the road and into the sandstorm. He quickly freed his ankles from the remaining rope.

Then, his clothing shredded into rags, his body burned and raked with bruises, his mind delirious, the Doomsday Warrior staggered toward the eye of the storm.

Chapter 3

They appeared on the horizon, twin pillars of black fire that Moses himself would have been proud to conjure. An eerie chill swept across the desert plains. It seemed as if the hand of God had come to arm-wrestle with the devil in Utah.

Rockson shielded his face against the stinging winds but was carried away like a piece of straw and dashed against a gravel-strewn slope. The force carried him roughly against the moving rocks for several yards before he was finally able to wedge himself between three large boulders. From his temporary sanctum, he peered through the cracks in the huge rocks. He could more sense than see the swirling monoliths in the distance. Then he knew. It was what the Indians called *Kala-Ka*, the "Battle of Winds."

First spawned in the holocaust of the great nuclear war, the *Kala-Ka* were violent upheavals of nature, storms marked by sinister double tornado funnels, often over 100,000 feet high, each spinning in opposite directions. They formed over the magnetic poles from impulses excited by intense irradiation of the earth's upper atmosphere. The spires acted as runaway generators, actually powering each other through a combination of magnetic force and atmospheric pressure. The *Kala-Ka* combined the most potent elements of a typhoon and a hurricane, and carried each to its furthest extreme. The twin towers would sweep across the terrain, spinning around each other wildly, wreaking destruction in wide swaths. Eventually, one of the funnels would achieve a sufficiently greater force than its counterpart, and engulf it. This combination of opposing forces created a cataclysmic explosion and a massive vacuum hundreds of miles square. Anything within its tracks would be instantly sucked into the center at speeds exceeding the speed of sound.

Indian legends were rich with tales of the storms. Some fanciful tales claimed that the storms were "Time-tornados"—tunnels in time! Whatever, they had never been known to occur below the Canadian Plains. This one had broken free and run down the North American continent, following the eastern ridge of the Rocky Mountains. What the heat of the desert would add to the storm's forces was anybody's guess. But Rock wasn't interested in finding out. All he knew was that the storm was here, and he intended to put as much distance between him and it as possible. He decided to try and make it back to the missile silo and take his chances with the Russians. But he wasn't giving himself very good odds.

Struggling to his feet, he looked out over the plain and witnessed an awesome phenomenon. The sands of the desert, billions upon billions of tons, were sucked into the eye of the storm. Oddly, visibility became crystal clear for miles as every bit of debris rose into the towering behemoths of the storm. The entire spectacle opened up before Rock's eyes, revealing, a theatrical performance on the universal scale. A drama of Nature gone mad.

It was clear that one of the twisters had grown noticeably larger than the other and was moving toward it, drawing in matter, charging it with electromagnetic force, and adding it to its hulking, oppressive power. Then Rock saw why the Indians called it the "Battle of Winds." He hung onto the boulders just out of the danger zone, about fifty miles away, as the show reached its climax.

The two murderous funnels began to circle each other in a macabre, titanic dance, slowly at first, then faster and faster until they were dancing twin stars, creating one giant funnel while an ear-splitting screech announced the imminent explosion. By now, the desert floor had become a sea of bedrock, stripped of every grain of sand. The sky was as clear as glass, as every speck of debris had been dragged into the dynamo, and the air was filled with lightning flashes.

Then, on the desert floor in the state of Utah, in the area once known as Monument Valley, Nature orchestrated her dramatic show of vengeance with savage fury and icy precision. In the flash of an instant, a massive vacuum formed and collapsed, polar and desert winds collided, billions of tons of charged debris crashed back to the earth . . . It seemed as if the Furies themselves ran wild across the range. A double-whammy of dynamic forces converged into a combined implosion-explosion. Rock looked back to kiss his ass good-bye as he was pulled up from his hiding place into the wild blue yonder.

Once engulfed within the pressurized magnetic field of the storm, Rock shed the puny force of gravity and encroached on another dimension. He felt himself spinning through space, yawing and tumbling, protected from collisions with other objects by a strong magnetic field that charged everything within the storm's eye, causing objects to repel each other. He was like a planet in deep space, unable to breath yet not needing air to live. All perceptions were twisted but he could sense objects floating alongside him, seemingly motionless but actually hurling with him at breakneck speeds in their own upward orbit. Images appeared like phantoms in his midst: parts of buildings, vehicles, people, horses, phasing in and out of his consciousness in a parade of surrealism. The bubble of silence burst with a cavernous roar, a sonic boom, the force undulating in waves through Rock's body.

He seemed to fall forever. He fell for so long that he began laughing and lashing about at the darkness all around him, not knowing whether he was dead or alive, falling to earth or to the bowels of hell.

When he finally stopped falling it was not with a bang but with a whimper. He landed on his feet, almost as if he'd jumped off a low roof, and his momentum carried him forward in a run. As he braked himself, the darkness ebbed, the terrible pressure lifted, and his eyes adjusted to the bright sun burning high in the midday sky. His ears popped.

But when he looked around him, instead of the desolate sandy plain and rocky buttes he expected, he found himself in the middle of a thriving metropolis.

He had barely arrested his forward motion when an automobile screeched by him only inches away, the driver leaning on the horn and cursing out the window. It was a red Toyota.

"Out of the road, you tramp!" he bellowed.

Rock, exhausted, drenched in a cold sweat, his shredded sealskin garb dangling from his tortured body in shreds, darted from the midst of the roadway he found himself on, while an endless stream of strange automobiles and trucks whizzed past, horns blaring, people scowling, the midday sun baking the asphalt tarmac. Where the hell was he?

He stood on a high bridge, the uppermost overpass of an elaborate cloverleaf intersection at the fringe of the great desert city. To his far right, a wide lake stretched to the horizon, the city crowding along its shores, crowned by an immense tower in its center. To the left, the desert opened as far as the eye could see.

Parched with thirst, his mind racing for coordinates, he began stumbling along the thin sidewalk leading past the rows of traffic to the ground. Rock struggled onward for half a mile before reaching a stranger who stood fuming over his overheated engine, tie loosened, sweat pouring from his pudgy face. Behind him a chorus of drivers cursed him for "blocking the lane."

"Got to hell . . ." he screamed to a greasy dude driving a racy yellow convertible. An *Oldsmobile*! Another antique vechicle!

Rockson stumbled up to the man as he slammed the hood down on his steaming engine.

"What . . . where . . . who?" Rockson mumbled.

The man looked up at the strange figure. "Huh?

Oh, listen, pal, I got troubles of my own today . . . Gimme a break and keep moving. You know the slogan, 'Don't Feed the Homeless!' "

"But . . . but . . ." Rockson gasped, gawking at the man's strange clothing and pointing around in a stupor.

"All right, all right, *here* . . ." said the stranger, shoving a U.S. one-dollar bill into Rock's hand and turning away. "Now beat it before you get picked up. I've got my own troubles. I got six buyers waiting for sixteen thousand feet of four-inch plastic pipe while I'm stuck with an overheated rental car in the middle of rush hour on a holiday weekend. Now we all got problems, pal, so beat it."

Rock continued on his way, his jaw hanging open, staring into the city as he approached, then at the screaming faces in the cars, then at the strange piece of green oblong paper the man had given him, studying the picture of the funny-looking white-haired old man in the middle. George Washington.

Chapter 4

Rockson staggered, bewildered, down the highway ramp onto a city street. The sun beat down without mercy on the concrete pavement. The air shimmered. Sweat poured down his face. God, what manner of place was this? Rockson stared in awe at the tall glass-and-concrete buildings that lined the broad avenues full of the hustle and bustle of a great city. He'd seen towns before that were large—but they were Soviet-occupied. And none were so populated as this. It was a veritable beehive of activity. The city actually hummed. It sounded, sometimes, like a song.

Traffic was relentless. The streets were filled with cars, trucks and buses heading pell-mell to their various destinations. The buses were the worst. Their exhaust filled the air with a malodorous blue haze that stung his nostrils and made Rockson choke and gag. He walked on, half in a daze.

Throngs of people filled the sidewalks, entering and exiting the various stores, restaurants, and supermarkets that advertised their wares in the windows.

Every now and then a group of people would gather at the streetcorners as if waiting for something. Suddenly the cars would stop as if by some prearranged signal and the people would cross in a group, and then the traffic would start up again. No one had time to answer his questions. At best they'd give him a funny look, but most walked by as if he weren't there.

The most popular stores, with bunches of citizens gathered in front of the windows, were the music stores. Everyone in this city seemed to love music. But music store was spelled *Muzik Store*.

Odd.

Numerous people were wearing headphones and would occasionally fiddle with small metallic boxes attached to their belts. Music tapes? And for those without headphones, there was always the canned music which poured forth from loudspeakers mounted atop every light pole. Rockson was getting annoyed. The city's din was largely caused by the homogenized rehash of ancient popular middle-of-the-road tunes.

He came to a restaurant called Happy Face. The sign in the window promised service with a smile. Rock pushed open the door and was greeted with a welcoming rush of cold air and the equally chilly smile of the hostess wearing a happy face pinned to the collar of her frosty-pink shirtwaist dress. "I'm afraid you'll have to leave, sir. You are not observing the proper dress code. All men must wear a tie and jacket."

Rockson looked around at the tables filled with people eating and drinking. There were businessmen

37

dressed in suits and ties, but there were also a number of other people wearing shorts and tee shirts. "Listen, I'm sorry about my clothes, but I just arrived in town and—well, my—plane crashed in the desert. All I really want is some water."

"I'll be right back," she responded. "Wait here," she pointed to a sign that said PLEASE WAIT TO BE SEATED. Her high heels clicked against the tile floor as she turned smartly and walked down the aisle. She disappeared through a swinging door at the back of the restaurant. Rockson waited as patiently as he could but the sight and smell of food and drink was overwhelming. The cashier stared at his every move. People were beginning to notice him and point. In a few minutes the hostess reappeared followed by a beefy sort of man—the manager?

"What seems to be the problem here?" asked the manager.

"There's no problem. I just want something to eat and drink. That's what a restaurant is for, isn't it?" Rockson was in no mood to parry with the manager.

"This establishment only caters to paying customers," the manager went on. "By law, we are not allowed to feed the homeless," he said, pointing to a sign that said NO BEGGARS ALLOWED. Before Rockson could say any more, he was pushed emphatically out of the restaurant onto the hot concrete.

A few stores down, Rockson tried a small corner grocery, and asked for a glass of water. In response to his question, the counterman sprayed him with a can of air freshener. "Get out of here! You stink!" Rockson had no choice but to leave. Best not to make a fuss until he found out his situation. He walked further into the city.

The stares he met from passersby grew steadily more hostile. The restaurants were fancier, with names like Le Posh Gourmet, or Organic Food Delicatessen. Signs were posted everywhere in front of new construction sites: *"Elegant, discriminating, exclusive condos filled with all the latest conveniences a modern career couple would want. No children or pets allowed."*

Snob city, Rockson thought.

Finally, exhausted, confused, hungry and thirsty, and oh so hot, he saw an area of green — Pioneer Park, according to the wooden sign. At least there might be a bench to sit down upon. Though most of the park's trees were dead and the grass parched brown, still, he was drawn to it like a magnet.

At the park's entrance was this sign: *"No ball playing, no skating, no cycling, no food vending, no littering, and Please Keep Off the Grass."* God, there were more signs telling you what you could or could not do than Rockson had ever seen. Nevertheless, he followed a path that led to a grassy knoll and sat on the cool dew-damp grass. The big red sun was beginning to set; the streetlights came on. Rockson felt that no one would see him as he lay down and stared into the tree branches around him. Mulling over the events of the day, he gradually became less aware of the noises and sights around him and then fell asleep.

He was rudely awakened by someone going through his pockets. Instinctively Rockson grabbed his assailant by the wrists. He heard a scream of pain.

"What are you doing?" demanded Rockson.

"Nothing," came a man's hoarse voice. "I just

wanted to see if you could spare some change."

"Change?" asked Rockson as he loosened his grip.

"Dimes, nickels, quarters—in short, money. Coin of the realm, so to speak," said the old man, breaking away and standing up. By the light Rockson could see that he was bald, had a long beard. And he was wearing an old smelly torn overcoat.

"What realm is this?"

"The U.S. of A., that's what. Where do you come from that you don't know that? You a foreigner? I ain't seen no foreigners for years."

"It's a long story. Let's just say I crashed in the desert." Rockson thought for a moment, and reached into his one remaining pocket and pulled out the wadded bill. "You mean this?"

The old man reached forward to swipe it out of Rockson's hand. "Now just hold on there, old-timer. Before I give you this, you'd better answer some questions." The old man eyed the bill hungrily.

"First, where are we? What city is this? Is it Red-controlled?

"Brother, this is Salt Lake City, biggest burg in Utah, U.S.A."

"Is this a Free city? How do you keep the Reds from blasting you all to hell?"

"I don't have any idea what you mean, citizen. Gimme the buck." He made another grab for it, but Rockson was faster.

"Not yet." Rock held it away from grasping hands.

The old man eyed Rockson quizzically. "You ask funny questions. But ask all the questions you want. I'm enjoying the game. You must be a recent home-less—right?"

40

Rockson was getting nowhere fast. The old man must be addled. He thought he would try one more time. "Where can a stranger get a bath—and a drink of water?"

"It'll cost you," the old man said, holding out his hand.

"All right, here." Rockson handed him the funny-looking piece of paper. The old man was as good as his word. He led him to a large fountain overlooking what looked like a plaza. Not exactly what he had in mind, but the fountain looked cool and inviting. Rockson couldn't resist the urge to jump in. What the hell, the cool water soothed his fevered brow, and more importantly he assuaged his thirst, cupping his hands and drinking. The old man stared at Rockson running like a wild man through the waters which sprayed from the mouths of marble seagulls. Suddenly he looked alarmed. "The rookies are coming!" he screamed, and then took to his heels.

Madder than a hatter, Rockson thought as he dove into the waters again. But when he emerged, he faced two machine guns held by men wearing red coveralls topped with mirror-visor helmets.

"Come on, derelict. Nice and easy. This fountain isn't the public bath. Get your ass over to the city dump, where you belong."

Rockson climbed sheepishly out of the pool. "Are you cops?" he asked.

"We're rookies," the tall one answered, pointing to his badge with a castle insignia. "Don't backtalk us. Murphy, let's run this one in."

"Put your hands in the air," said the one called Murphy. He held his gun on Rockson while the tall one frisked him, sneering in hatred. Why?

"It's okay. He's unarmed," said the tall rookie. He stared at Rockson and asked, "Got a name, bum?"

"My name is Ted Rockson. I'm an American. A Freeman."

Murphy snapped up his visor and squinted at Rock. "The name sounds familiar . . . Yeah, maybe I know you. We'd better take you down to headquarters and run you through R and I. Get you home. I recognize you now."

"R and I?"

"Research and Information." Rockson was handcuffed and escorted to a shiny red Toyota Camry with PATROL written on its door idling at the corner. Rockson had hardly climbed into the back seat when the door slammed and they took off like a rocket. Within a few minutes they were at the station house, a sooty concrete-slab gray building.

"Got a drunk citizen," said the taller of the two rookies to the desk clerk. "We caught him playing in the fountain. Can you believe it? Right now he looks like a good candidate for *Twenty Questions*."

"He's not the only one. We've got a full house tonight. Must be a full moon," the desk clerk laughed. The tall rookie sat Rockson on a bench and started typing up an officer's arrest report.

"All right. Take him down to Psychiatry," the clerk added as he took the typewritten form from the rookie and handed him back his carbon copy.

Rockson was fingerprinted, photographed, and booked. Then he was turned over to a consultant, a pale silent man wearing a blue blazer with a chess king emblazoned on his pocket.

The consultant said, "Stand up," and waved his long thin stick ominously. The tip of the metal rod flickered red. A weapon?

Rockson was led down a staircase, and through a long corridor. At the end of the tiled white hall, was a door. The sign on the door stated, *Roy G. Biv, Psychiatrist*. The consultant opened the door for Rockson, and he was shoved into a chair. Rockson's natural tendency when shoved around was to shove back. But somehow he knew that would be futile—if not deadly. He sat back in the cool leatherette and faced the man behind the desk. The man was reading something, but he put it down. He stared at Rockson a long time through his thick round wire-rim glasses. The man had a gray beard and looked like Freud.

At last the psychiatrist spoke. "Do you know why you're here?"

"They said I was drunk," Rockson said.

The psychiatrist stood up, walked around the desk, and leaned over so close to Rock's face he could smell the Binaca. "Weren't you drunk? What were you doing in the Seagull fountain?"

"I was thirsty. And hot."

"Hmmmmmmm. Do you always wear such—unusual—clothes?"

"Not usually. But I was up in Alaska. An Eskimo gave it to me."

"Hmmmmmmmmmm." The shrink circled the desk again, sat down, wrote on a piece of paper. Then he looked up again. "Well, now. What *shall* we do with you?"

The consultant smiled. "He needs music. This man is Theodore Rockman, C.P.A.—a solid citizen according to records. He must be drunk. Perhaps his ears got clogged up and he didn't hear the music and got confused."

"Hmmmmm. That is exactly my diagnosis, Consultant. Let us take him to the music room. Give him some easy listening for a night."

That didn't sound so awful a sentence, Rock thought. The consultant told him to stand, and, waving his long red-tipped rod in a menacing way, directed the Doomsday Warrior back upstairs.

The man took him to a large bare-walled room with shower stalls at one end and a set of small barred cells at its other end. There were two Rookies there, visors up, smoking. They quickly doused their cigarettes and saluted when the consultant came in with him.

The consultant turned him over to the two, directing them to have Rockson "listen to the music." Then the blue-blazered man left. The rookies took out another couple of cigarettes and lit up. They eyed Rockson with some amusement as he stood there. Rockson thought about grabbing for their guns — until he saw the cameras at both ends of the room swing and lock onto him. Someone else was watching — he'd have no chance of escape. The door only opened with a buzz from some other location anyway — there was no doorknob.

He was told to strip and shower — which he was eager to do anyway. While he was toweling dry, the rookies started jabbering.

"Do you believe this outfit?" exclaimed the heavy-set rookie, picking up Rockson's tattered sealskin parka with a pair of tongs and throwing it into a bin.

"Give him some prisoner's coveralls, Johnson."

As soon as Rockson slipped the coveralls on and zipped them, he was then unceremoniously thrown into a jail cell.

Rockson sat down on the small cot, the only object in the nine-by-twelve room except for the toilet and a small sink. The walls were cinder-block, unpainted gray. The ceiling was low and had several strainerlike speakers that music—the dreadful music that seemed to permeate the city—sifted down from. Within a few minutes, a little dinner in a three-compartment aluminum hot tray and a cup of coffee were shoved through a slot in the door. He fell on it like a ravenous wolf.

Things could be worse, he thought as he sipped the last dregs of his coffee. He was clean, wearing comfortable clothes, and he wasn't hungry or thirsty anymore. But he *was* in jail. They had just laughed when he'd told them he was Ted Rockson, the Doomsday Warrior. Laughed when he asked which way to Colorado. Why?

He had to think, organize what he had seen and heard in this weird city, and draw some conclusions. First, this had to be an American city. He hadn't seen a single Soviet around. Second, it was awfully primitive—reciprocating engine vehicles, high-rise buildings—and that luncheonette! Straight out of *history books*!

That was it. The whole place, the name of the city even, was straight out of a *history book*. The storm! The storm had lifted him up and— Why, it must have thrown him back in time. It was impossible, and yet what other conclusion could he draw? He had once

45

passed the area that once held the ancient Salt Lake City. . . .

He had been on a mission back in 2089, in this very same area. And there hadn't been a trace of the vast city. It didn't exist in the twenty-first century. It had been nuked, along with most other cities. And yet here he was, sitting in a cell in the heart of Salt Lake City.

Time travel! No wonder they thought he'd been babbling. They didn't know of Freefighters, nor of the Soviet occupation of America; nor about the Doomsday Warrior or Century City. Because it *hadn't happened yet.*

Assuming he was right, what year *was* it? How would he find out? *Ask!*

He banged on the bars. "Hey, officer," he yelled to the uniformed man down the hall who was leaning his chair against the wall reading a newspaper. "What's today's date?"

The man put down his paper. "Oh, you're coming out of your drunk, huh? Want to know what day it is? Well, it's Wednesday."

"Wednesday *what*?"

The cop laughed. That drunk, huh? Wednesday, September sixth." He lifted up his paper. "Go back to sleep, citizen."

"One more thing," Rockson asked. "Could I have a look at the paper when you're done?"

"Sure . . ." But the officer kept reading. He wasn't done.

Rockson sat on the cot for another twenty minutes before he heard the wooden chair creak. The cop sauntered up to the cell and passed the large paper through the bars. "Gulls swatted the Locusts, eleven to five," he said.

"Wow," said Rockson, not knowing what the hell that meant. He tried to contain himself. He waited till the cop went back down the hall before he started looking over the paper. Sports section — it was turned to the sports section. He folded it back to page one. It was the *Salt Lake Herald*, price forty cents. Headline, LUMBINI PEACE TALKS ON. Date. *Date!* Oh, my God! September 6, *1989*. A hundred and three years before Rockson had been swept up in the *Kala-Ka*, storm of storms.

And the headline — Lumbini? Why, that's the big conference center, set up in Nepal in the late 1980s. The place the nuclear powers tried to work out their differences — before the nuke war. The nuke war started on September 11, 1989. *Five days from today*. Rockson gasped. Unless he got the hell out of this city, he'd be dead meat in *five days*.

He pounded on the cell bars, scraped his metal cup against them. He made a lot of noise but no one was in the corridor. Soon the lights dimmed. He was there for the night, and they expected him to sleep.

But, how can you sleep when you expect to be vaporized in days?

The music, rather than dying down, increased in volume. He tried to find some control that would turn it down, but to no avail. The sound seemed to vibrate his teeth; he could feel his ribs shaking. It was getting so loud that he couldn't stand it. The music resonated, bouncing from the bare concrete walls. The bass was so deep that the cot started shaking on every drumbeat. The highs were distorted to an ear-piercing screech.

"Stop!" Rockson yelled. "Stop the music!" He held his hands against his tortured ears, but the music penetrated. His eyes hurt, his head throbbed. And he slumped to the floor unconscious.

"Had a good night's rest, citizen?" Rockson looked up from the floor. His eyes focused upon a red uniform—a rookie was shaking him awake. "Bet you feel better now, citizen. Everything is back in its place."

Rockson sat up and rubbed his eyes. "*What a dream*," he said. "I—thought I was out on the desert, fighting—soldiers—and then a storm came and—and—something. I can't remember. Wow, I've got a splitting headache. Where am I?"

"In the drunk tank, citizen. You really tied one on. You looked so bad that we thought you were a homeless. From Sadtown. But Murphy remembered you. He lives on your block. We ran your prints and pic through the records. And we called your wife. She's bailed you out. Stand up, it's time to go home, Rock."

Rockson stood up, aided by the rookie. He was unsteady on his feet. The pleasant music coming out of the ceiling speakers soothed him; it made him feel pleasantly comfortable. He liked it.

"Do you know your name, citizen?"

Rock said, "Sure, Ted Rockson."

The rookie laughed. "You mean Rockman—right?"

Rockson rubbed his matted hair again. "Rockman?

48

Yeah, Rockman. Sorry."

"Okay, I guess you're presentable enough. Your wife will be in in a moment." The rookie went out, leaving the cell door open.

Wife? In a few minutes his question was answered when he heard a familiar voice say, ". . . and I'll take good care of him, officer. I won't let it happen again."

"Kim? Boy, am I glad to see you," said Rockson as the blue-eyed blonde entered. She gave him a perfunctory kiss and then frowned.

"You'd *better* be glad. Here, put this on," Kim said, handing him a fresh suit. "I've been so worried about you. You've been missing since Monday night. I try to be a good wife to you, and this is the thanks I get, Mr. Man-about-town! Can't trust you for a minute. You said something about getting ice cream. When you didn't return I thought you'd been kidnapped. Then I get this call saying you were picked up on a drunk-and-disorderly charge running around in the Seagull fountain! They showed me the outfit you were running around in—I nearly died of shame. I told them to burn it. If anyone we know saw you like that, your career would be ruined."

Rockson let her rattle on while he changed his clothes. Then he leveled with her. "Kim, I can't quite remember clearly. . . Are you sure you're my wife?"

She softened. "Oh, darling, you *are* in bad shape. Here—your nose must have been bleeding. Are you all right?" She dabbed at his upper lip, kissed him on the cheek, and straightened his tie. "Come on, let's go home. I can't let the neighbor watch the kids so much without paying her. And you're already lost two days' pay this week."

Kids? "How are the—kids?" Rockson asked as they walked down the long corridor to the lobby. Why was he so woozy?

"They're fine. You ought to thank your lucky stars that the chess tournament started this week. They've been positively glued to the TV. I don't think they really noticed you were gone. Ted junior *did* want to know if you would show him how to use his new weed-burner, and Barbara—well, you know how girls are."

"Right."

"I'll drive," said Kim, taking out her keys. "In your condition you probably wouldn't even know the way home," she laughed. She got behind the wheel of a rusty green Gremlin parked in front of the police station.

"What an antique!' Rock exclaimed as he climbed in and slammed the door.

"You're telling me," Kim said as she put the key in the ignition. Instantly the radio began blaring and a horrible whining sound began.

"Don't forget to buckle up, dear." Rockson did as he was told and the whining sound ceased. "Let's see. First stop—*Cheaps*."

As she put her foot to the floor, the car sputtered and jumped. They left the police station trailing a cloud of blue smoke.

Cheaps turned out to be a sprawling supermarket on the outskirts of town with its own large parking lot. NOW OPEN 24 HOURS, a bright-red neon sign proclaimed.

"I think tonight should be special, don't you?" Kim

50

said as she parked the car. "I want to get a steak, and I can't forget to get some Ruffy dog food. Just ran out this morning. You just wait in the car, dear. I'll be right back," she said. She slammed the door.

Rockson thought he must have amnesia. He couldn't remember anything. His head throbbed. I must have been really looped, he thought. I feel so muzzy. Wife? Children? Dog? The radio blared on. Well, Kim is real anyway. He recognized her. It must be true. Can't argue with facts. In a few minutes Kim returned with a bag of groceries and tossed it in the back seat. Moments later they were off again trailing a cloud of blue smoke.

Home was an apartment building on Southeast 10th Street. Rock waited in front of it with the groceries, trying to get his bearings while Kim parked the car. "We're in luck," she said when she returned. "I found a spot just around the corner." She unlocked the door and Rock followed her up to the stairs to the fourth floor. They were greeted at the apartment door by Ted junior, who was wearing red coveralls with a mirrored visor helmet, carrying a toy flamethrower. He looked to be about six.

"Stop in the name of the law, or I'll cremate ya," he said pulling the trigger of his toy weed-burner. White sparks came out of it. Rock jumped involuntarily, backing against the wall.

"That was good, Daddy," the boy laughed, as more sparks came out of the burner. "Let's do it again."

"Daddy's tired, honey. You can show him your knight outfit after dinner," Kim said, leading the way through the crowded living room into the kitchen. "Barbara, I want you to pick up that chess set and

51

take it into your room. Skippy—Skippy, *get off* the paper!" The dog barked and jumped down from the comfortable, familiar-looking overstuffed chair.

Rock stood in the kitchen door as Kim put away the groceries. "It's the overwork that did this to you. You're such a hard-working husband."

"Yes, maybe I am a bit overtired. Thanks for putting up with me. I know I've been acting—"

"Oh, Rock," she said, crushing her soft body against him, "you'll be fine in the morning. You probably haven't eaten much of anything for a couple of days. I'll give you a nice steak dinner in just a jiff, as soon as the microwave heats it up." She smiled her big blues at Rockson. "You shouldn't have to worry about tomorrow morning. I phoned your boss and said that you needed a couple of days' rest—that you were sick due to all that overwork. He was very understanding. He said he hated to do without you because of all the accountants under him, that you were the very best. Maybe you'll get that promotion real soon, after all." She took him by the hand and led him into the living room. "Why don't you put on your slippers and read the condo ads," she suggested as she picked up the paper. "Don't the State Street Co-ops sound fabulous?" she asked. Kim handed him the real-estate section of the *Evening Herald*. She clapped her hands together. "Come on, Skippy, time for din-din. Ruff! Ruff!" The dog jumped down from the easy chair and, barking joyfully, ran after her into the kitchen.

Rockson sat down in his "favorite" chair, shucked off his shoes, and slipped his feet into the velveteen slippers—a perfect fit. Of course, because they're mine, he thought. He stared at the full page ad. *Grand Opening of the State Street Towers. Over 70 %sold. Over a hundred floors of the most exciting, exclusive apartments to grace downtown Salt Lake City in years. John Bowles, builder makes a BIG Statement on State Street. His interiors are the State-of-the-Art. Don't miss this fabulous opportunity to look down on your fellow man. Don't be afraid to move up to State Street.*

In smaller print it read, *Apartments from $499,000, 10% APR.* On the bottom of the page in the largest letters yet it read, *The sky's the limit!*

Rockson didn't know what to make of this. How could he possibly afford such an apartment? Kim did have a point about their living in cramped living quarters.

He looked around the overfurnished apartment. In the ten-by-twelve-foot living room was the pink morris chair he sat in, a red velvet love seat full of plastic dog toys, a large console TV—Motorola? Then there were two end tables holding giant plastic-shaded lamps that were in the shape of flamingos. Track spotlights on the ceiling shone on the several paintings on velvet, depicting big-eyed, sad children, that were tacked to the wall. Underfoot was a dog-haired shag rug.

He picked up the news section of the *Post-Dispatch* on the floor. PEACE TALKS GOING WELL read the headline. That's good, he thought, reading on. *Thursday, September 7 (AP). The peace talks at Lumbini, Nepal World Peace Center, under the auspices of the U.N., are going well, according to Douglas Sweig, Asst. U.S. delegate to the conference. Sweig reports that the Soviet Union and China have agreed in principle to the U.S. proposal to reduce, by 23% a year, the nuclear stockpiles that have accumulated over the past 45 years. By 1993 each state will have only 8% of its current arsenal of ICBMs, SLBMs, and IRBMs. The Soviet Union has also agreed in principle to the U.S.–Chinese proposal that Japan be allowed to develop a small nuclear capability strictly for peaceful purposes, and to maintain security in its worldwide trading zone.*

Rockson smiled. Everyone is agreeing, all is well. He sighed and tried to relax his muscles. The soothing music drifting from the stereo set over the dresser was helping dispel some of the tensions — the smell of the steak from the kitchen, the gentle humming of Kim along with the music; "Don't let the stars get in your eyes," was the refrain. The kids were in their room, probably quietly playing like they always did. The dog was half asleep at his feet. All was well.

Rockson picked up the newspaper again. He glanced at the date: *Thursday, September 7, 1989.* Something seemed odd about that.

He put the paper down, "Kim? Could you come in here?"

Kim came out of the kitchen. "What did you say, dear?"

"What date is it?" Rockson asked. "Is this right? Look at this newspaper."

She took the paper from his hand and read, "Thursday, September seventh. That's right, dear. Why? Did you think it was Wednesday?"

Rockson smiled, "Yeah. I guess I did. . . . Funny, isn't it?"

"Really, dear, the *Herald* never makes a mistake. It's been Thursday all day!"

Rockson closed his eyes, "Of course. Guess I should rest. . . . Thanks, dear."

"Mistakes happen." She smiled, and winked.

Chapter 5

"There's the bell on the microwave; the synthosteak is ready, dear! You sit still; I'll roll in the TV table, and you can eat and watch *Twenty Questions* with me snuggled against your knee. Oh, Rock, I've been so happy these past few years—since our marriage."

TV? Rock looked up at the make-believe Spanish-oak cabinet with the big greenish screen. TV. That was a good idea. He went over and turned on the switch. He sat back in his chair and watched the screen brighten. A commercial came on. *"Ruffy dog food is good for your pet."*

"Ruffy, Ruffy," said the black-and-white pooch. Rockson smiled. How the hell *do* they do that? *"This is KREK in Salt Lake City, Channel Two. Stay tuned for* TWENTY QUESTIONS."

The logo of a spinning word that blew apart to form the words "Twenty Questions" came upon the screen in a dazzle of color.

"And now your host, Jeri Jet!" The smiling emcee, a twentyish thin man with gold hair, in a pink suit, came on the screen. *"Good day to you all out there in TV Land . . . Are you ready to play* Twenty Ques-

tions?"

"Yes!" came the roar of approval from an unseen audience.

"Well, let's go! Now, for our first *contestant!"* said Jeri Jet, stepping aside. The vermilion curtain parted, and a naked man trussed to a chair appeared. He looked a lot like the derelict who had led Rockson to the fountain the other day—a coincidence, no doubt. The man had electrical wires taped to his ankles.

Jeri Jet walked over, leaned down at the man in the chair, and said, *"Contestant, are you ready for* Twenty Questions?"

The man cried out *"No!"* but was overwhelmed by the roar of *"Yes!"* from the audience.

Rockson leaned forward, intensely interested. Kim came into the room rolling the synthosteak and broccoli out on the TV tray. She sat down beside him on the floor, *"Oooh*, has it started?" she asked.

Rock said nothing. His knuckles were white; his hands gripped the plush arms of the chair. What the hell was this?

"First question," said Jeri Jet, jabbing a finger at the man. *"What are you for?"*

"I'm for freedom!"

"WRONG!" Jeri Jet yelled, and his hand dropped down. The contestant suddenly convulsed as if electricity had shot along the wires leading to his body. For an instant, his tangled, black hair stood on end.

"Is that a jolt of electricity?" Rock asked.

Kim laughed. "Don't be silly—it's just special effects. Nothing is real on TV."

"The correct answer is . . ." Jet smiled. The audience yelled *"SOCIAL ORDER."*

"SECOND QUESTION," Jeri Jet yelled. "What are you for?"

The man in the chair looked around wildly, said nothing. Jeri Jet repeated the question. Kim squeezed Rockson's knee, "The answer is social order, everyone knows that," she said. "Come on, come on!"

Another convulsion swept through the naked bound man. He struggled to free himself.

"We're waiting," laughed Jeri Jet. "What's your answer?" The man on the chair spat and said, "Rock 'n roll."

"WRONG!" yelled the audience—and Kim.

The contestant's hair stood on end and again he started convulsing. He slumped, his body limp.

Jeri Jet turned solemnly to the camera. "And now, the voice of our beloved leader, with a message for today!"

The screen faded, and replacing the gruesome quiz program was a drawing of a red chess piece—the king. A strong male voice bellowed out, "Don't give to the beggars and street people. Citizens, you work hard for your money. Let the loafers and deviants starve if they don't want to work. I, the chessman respect you . . . Respect you."

The voice-over was repeated twice. The logo of the chess king with the superimposed words SOCIAL ORDER was spinning, faster and faster, until it was a spiral. Then it faded.

Kim sighed. "He's so wonderful."

Rockson wasn't listening to her. Where? Where had he heard that voice before? Not in this city, not on television. Where?

Then the quiz program was back. Rockson watched

tensely as *"THIRD QUESTION!"* was yelled by the audience. *"No!"* begged the man on the chair. *"No, please don't ask."*

"YES," yelled the audience. Kim squeezed Rockson's left calf. "Isn't it exciting? Can we make love after the program, dear?"

Rockson mumbled, "Yes, of course," and continued to watch the glaring screen. *"THIRD QUESTION,"* shouted Jeri Jet. *"What are you for?"*

The man on the chair cried out, *"Social order, goddamn it."*

Jeri Jet exclaimed, *"Correct! Martha, the man has given the correct answer. Let's see what he's won!"* A slender woman in a white-sequined see-through gown came out and another curtain opened. The audience oooed and aahed as *"Fabulous kitchen appliances"* passed in front of them. *"A washer/dryer, a blender, a new microwave. Total value twelve thousand dollars and one cent,"* Jeri Jet concluded.

The contestant was cut loose and led away weeping, by slinky Martha.

"MORE," Jeri Jet shouted, *"after this message."*

While the dog food commercial barked on, Rockson asked Kim, "What happens if they don't answer correctly?"

"They have twenty tries at the question. If they don't answer correctly by their twentieth try, they don't win the kitchen."

"How are they selected to be on the program?"

"Why, I don't know, dear. Does it matter?"

"No, I guess not . . ."

Jeri Jet's "More" turned out to be a wiggle from Martha, a wave good bye from Jeri, and another station logo.

"Finish your meal, dear—it's time to turn it off and go to bed," said Kim. "I want to show you my new negligee outfit—it's super."

In a few minutes he had cleaned the plate off. She cooked well.

Rockson followed her into the bedroom, which consisted almost entirely of a double-sized bed and wall and ceiling mirrors. The only other furniture besides the immense bed was a small dresser and some of those big-eyed-children paintings. Rockson wondered why the bedroom didn't seem familiar at all.

"Did you redecorate, Kim?"

"No, silly. Now you wait here a second, while I go in the bathroom and put on my new outfit. . . ."

Rock sat down on the red velour bedspread. The bed jiggled, it felt cool. He pulled the sheets off one end—rubber. It was a water bed. He lay down. It rocked back and forth, like he was in a rowboat.

"Take a look, dear. What do you think?"

Kim sure looked good—she was nearly naked, and the sepia-colored almost-transparent clingy bikini panties and push-up bra accentuated her curves. Her alabaster-complected skin seemed to glow softly in the lamplight. All the more so when Kim undulated her body over to the light switch and made an adjustment. The room's lighting turned a dim pink. "Maybe now you're ready for a little fooling around."

"Maybe so," Rock said. He felt his manhood solidifying. Kim had climbed up on the bed and undid his shirt buttons and unbuckled his pants. Then she unzipped him. He started to fondle her breasts but she said, "No!" slapping his hands and frowning. "No. First I do this," she said softly. She got down on her elbows and her cool white hands extracted his erect manhood from his pants. She engulfed it with her wet lips, bringing an immediate groan of pleasure from Rockson. "Just lie back, dear. Remember what the Chessman says about sex. It's the woman's job. After a hard day, the best thing is a blow job."

Rockson didn't protest; still, he wanted to hold her, run his fingers through her silky blond tresses. But every time he made a move to touch her, she objected. He lay back resigned to a passive role.

Kim's marshmallow-soft, pink lips continued to slide moistly up and down his manly staff, tightening ever so slightly now and then, bringing paroxysms of response from her bedmate.

Rockson could no longer remain idle. He pulled her face to his, stared at her. His eyes melted into her. "Kim, lie down. I'll do some of the moving—"

"But Chessman says—"

It was too late. Rockson had rolled over onto her, tearing the flimsy panties off with one snap of his fingers. He felt her yielding, her legs opening, her burning-hot sex wet and ready for him. "Yes . . . yes. Please, please *put it in*!"

Rockson needed no encouragement. It was a bit distracting to see endless rows of naked Rockson-Kim images—the damned mirrors—all around them, but soon he was lost in the task at hand. She undulated the wet tip of her blond triangle forward to meet his manhood, and he plunged.

He thought the shout that Kim uttered at that

instant might arouse the neighbors: *"Oh, yes, yes — Aaahhhh!"*

But soon she settled back to simple gasps and groans, punctuated by love-words. The probing staff slid in and out between the opened petals of flesh. She rolled her eyes, rocked her head back and forth on the pillow. The bed set up some sort of obscene rhythm underneath them. She moved up and down, meeting the Doomsday Warrior's every thrust, locking herself against him, being a full participant in the age-old ritual of coming together.

"Oh, it's so good. Oh, Rock, it's — been so long. I've — I've never — experienced you like this before. . . ."

"Don't talk — not now," he whispered. For he was reaching the point of explosive completion. Like a gathering tidal wave, he moved faster and faster, the mattress nearly bursting a seam from the impacts. At the same time, Kim was reaching her own peak. Then suddenly, together, they shuddered in surrender to the heaving ecstacy.

"Always, always I will love you," she said. She lay limp on the tousled satin sheets, exhausted as she had never been before. And happier.

Rockson was exhausted too. But when Kim turned off the love-light's pink rays, no matter how he tried, he couldn't sleep. He turned to look at Kim, his wife. She was beautiful.

She lay there asleep, a smile a mile wide on her face.

He sat up. Something still seemed wrong. He had

to think, *had to think*.

He went to sit near the bedroom window. He stared out over the humming city and the winking stars above.

Why? Why do I feel like a stranger in this city?

When Rock finally returned to bed it was four A.M. He dozed off; a dream began. It was a vivid, frightening thing, a nightmare of twisting images and symbols . . .

He was walking alone, walking across a long flat plain. Where was he going? Something about the mountains to the south . . . A vehicle appeared—a jeep. And in the jeep were red-clad men who laughed and pointed at him. They threw ropes, and though he fought with all his might the ropes ensnared him, like huge winding snakes; they coiled about his body, tightening. Then he was thrown down a hole, and as he screamed out *"Let me go, let me go,"* the snakes whirled him so that he spun on his heels like a top, around and around, and he couldn't stop.

Then a red-clad man came in, his face leered at Rockson every time he spun past the man. Then the spinning stopped and Rockson was on a big chessboard, and the red-clad man with the leer was wearing a crown, and Rockson felt on top of his head and he had a crown on also. And Rockson noticed that he was now dressed in a white outfit.

The man at the far end of the chessboard—it was a half-mile square, at least—was approaching. He came rapidly, without moving his feet. Rockson turned and tried to run, for he knew that something awful was about to happen. But he was blocked. Two men with flamethrowers, also dressed in red, were coming at him from the opposite direction, leering, spurts of fire coming from their weapons.

Rockson tried to run another way, but a beautiful blond woman with long wavy hair and blue eyes stopped him. She had no weapon, but her blue eyes flashed at him, and somehow they paralyzed him. Her mouth moved, her luscious lips undulated up and down, but he couldn't make out the words. What was she saying? Her body was all curves and she was dancing as she walked, swaying in her clinging white gown, which sparkled like starfields afire. The sexual rhythm of her movement was all-powerful, all-desirable. And Rockson couldn't break away from her spell, couldn't leave the square he stood upon, even though the two men with flamethrowers approached closer, even though the king in red was rapidly closing on him.

"*Stop*," Rockson shouted. "*Stop! Let me go, Kim, let me go!*"

Gasping for air that would not come, Rockson sat bolt-upright in bed and looked wildly around. The nightmare vision faded like an old sepia photograph in sunlight, until it was replaced by the room. And Kim was looking in his eyes, her mouth moving. "What's wrong, dear? Have you been having a nightmare? Do you want me to turn on the lamp?"

Rockson nodded; he could breath now, he could move. But he wanted to see the room better, wanted to know this wasn't also part of the nightmare. She

64

turned the light on, and Rockson, taking long oxygen-sucking breaths, looked around. There were the large-eyed-children pictures, the door to the bathroom, the bureau and mirrors. He was home, he was safe. His shoulders relaxed. He slid back down and put his hands, which had been in front of him in a defensive position, back down.

"I'm all right," he said. "Turn off the light. Let's go back to sleep. It was just a nightmare."

Chapter 6

Rockson awoke to the buzz of the alarm, the whistle of the kettle, and the sound of music. Moments before, he had been dreaming of something about being trapped by snakes, trudging endlessly in the desert. The combined sounds drove the rest of the dream from his head. He stared quietly at the ceiling. It'd seemed so real. He yawned. What day was it? Who was he? Where was he? Slowly it all came back to him. He was Ted Rockman, C.P.A. His eyes scanned the room. He was at home. Today was Friday, September eighth. He glanced at the clock — if he didn't hurry, he'd be late for work.

He swung himself out of bed, afraid it would collapse from the movement. His back ached. What a nightmare he'd had!

Kim's side of the bed was empty. He could hear her elsewhere in the apartment, humming along with the synthesized music that seemed to come from everywhere and couldn't be shut off.

Groggy, he shuffled into the bathroom and relieved himself, only to find the toilet didn't flush. The handle came off in his hand. For some reason he felt very dissatisfied, almost angry—at everything.

"Kim!" Rockson shouted. "Come look at this!"

Kim came to the doorway of the bathroom. She was wearing a pink chenille robe with a frilly green apron over it. She carried a fork, which she brandished like a weapon. "Yes, dear?" Before he could speak, she clucked, "The stove keeps going out. I'll have to run down to Worthington's and order a new one. I hope they're on sale."

He looked at her. She looked so stupid—what she wore was so silly too. It was some sort of tunic outfit that was a washed-out pink.

"What is it, dear?" Kim prodded him. "The Poptarts will burn if I don't get back to the kitchen."

"Poptarts."

"Why, yes, your tummy's favorite breakfast. Really, Teddy, you act like you never heard of Poptarts before."

Remembering his original point, Rockson indicated the toilet. "It's broken."

She sighed. "You'll have to call the repairman again. Speedfix takes care of all the maintenance." She pursed her lips in thought. "Except, I don't know if we have any money for plumbers, Teddy. Honestly, if you'd only go to Mr. Cooper and ask for a raise, like you promised. I'd like to buy some new furniture, too. . . . You think I enjoy looking at this third-rate stuff all day when we could have first-rate plastic on a better salary?"

"But—"

Just then the music swelled, snapping his patience. "Turn off that blasted music! I can't take it anymore!"

Kim looked as though he had slapped her in the

67

face. "Teddy, that's blasphemous! It's a crime! I'll pretend I didn't hear that! Oh, thank goodness the children already left for school — what a bad example you set!"

Rockson charged out of the bathroom, looking for a speaker or amplifier to punch out of commission. "I guess I'm just in a bad mood."

Kim burst into tears. Rockson halted, chagrined. He could not bear to see women cry. He went to her and said, "What's the matter?"

"You," bawled his wife. "You're not normal anymore. You say illegal things and you have such a temper! I'll have to turn you back over to the police. Then the kids and I will starve. We won't be able to pay our rent, and we'll get thrown out — We'll have to sleep on the streets —"

He shushed her. *"All right."* He would not mention the music again — he had no desire to have another run-in with the police. He only wanted to get out of the house. It was the nightmare; it had made him uneasy.

"I'm sorry," Rockson said, brushing away her tears.

She sniffed. "You'd better hurry and eat your breakfast, so you can get to work on time."

Work? He knew he was a C.P.A. — but what was a C.P.A.? Odd thoughts, disjointed memories, were sweeping over him like a tide going out to sea, and it was all he could do to not drown in them.

"I'm not going to work today," he said. "I have . . . other things to do."

Kim looked stricken again. "Teddy, you *must*. It's against the law to miss more than five days of work a year, and you've already missed several, thanks to your

68

little escapade. The police will know if you don't show up today, and I couldn't bear to go down to the detention-and-rehabilitation center and bail you out again."

She was already marshalling him back to the bedroom, pulling clothes out of a closet, and laying them on the bed. "Here, I pressed your best suit. Don't forget to be careful when you eat lunch — you always manage to spill something on your tie, and this one's brand new — I got it in a terrific sale at Harvey's — real silk, Teddy."

She waved a strip of red fabric at him. "And above all, *don't* say anything at work about being arrested. Why, I'd just *die* of disgrace to have everyone find out about it. I told the office you took time off to rest, that you were exhausted from working so hard — I figured it would play up the fact that you are such a hard worker . . ." Kim prattled on.

Done whipping clothes out of the closet and drawers, she hurried back to the kitchen as Rockson began to get dressed. "Oh, no!" he heard her wail. "The poptarts burned!"

Rockson sighed to himself. "It's all right — I'm not hungry," he muttered.

When he finished dressing, he stared at his distorted reflection in the cheap, ripply mirror. What a trussed-up outfit — fake-leather black shoes that pinched his feet, a gray suit that was tight across the shoulders, a stiff white shirt so tight at the neck that it practically choked off his air — how could any man be comfortable? How could any man *think* in clothes like this? No wonder there was talk of nuclear war. The men who owned the buttons had all the oxygen cut off from their brains from self-strangulation.

Kim bustled back into the bedroom, bearing a tall glass of red juice and a mug of coffee. "Here's your tomato juice and coffee, sweetie," she cooed. She set them down on the nightstand by the bed. "My, don't you look handsome in that suit! Here, let me do your tie — you never could do Windsor knots very well."

She slipped the tie under his collar and deftly cinched it up to Rockson's Adam's apple. He gagged.

"There! You look marvelous! My handsome Teddy!"

He gulped down the juice and coffee. He wanted to get out of the apartment as fast as possible before she killed him.

At the door, Kim pecked him on the cheek and thrust eight dollars into his hand. "It's almost all the money I have until you bring home your paycheck," she said accusingly. "Don't spend it all on lunch!" At Rockson's bewildered look, she went on, "Oh, you're still in a fog, aren't you? The police warned me this might happen. Here." She went to one of the glass tables, supported by two plastic cocker spaniels, and scrawled out some information on a scrap of paper.

Her voice took on a baby-talk tone, as though she were addressing a child. "Take the Number Four bus at the stop right outside our building, and get off at the sixth stop, which is Number One Nietzsche Square. That's your office building. I'm sure you'll find your way from there."

She handed him a fake-leather briefcase and pushed him out the door. "Have a good day, dear!"

70

As soon as her husband was gone, Kim's happy demeanor changed abruptly to sadness. She sat down in one of the bean-bag chairs and sniffled. Something had happened to Teddy, and she couldn't understand what. He just wasn't *himself* anymore. She ruminated over the events of the past few days.

It had all started four days ago, when Ted had gone out for a quart of ice cream—and disappeared. Kim had looked everywhere for him, to no avail. The next thing Kim had known, the police were calling her to come and get her husband, who'd been charged with drunk-and-disorderly conduct. She was shocked to the bone—Teddy had been a straight arrow his entire life.

She'd brought him home, but he hadn't been the same since. He acted like part of his memory was missing. Familiar things were strange to him, and he said the oddest things about the date and the TV programs. Mad things.

He seemed to be hallucinating. Poor Teddy! Was he going insane? Such things *did* happen. And what would become of her and the children if Teddy was put away?

She resolved to act normal. Teddy would come around and return to his usual self. Except for one thing: He had mysteriously become a great lover. She hoped *that* change would endure!

The morning air was already hot, adding to Rockson's discomfort in the ill-fitting clothes and shoes. At the bus stop, he bought a newspaper, looking for

71

answers to the questions that overwhelmed him. The date on the paper disturbed him: September 8, 1989.

That damned nightmare had blown a few of his circuits!

Why was the date frightening? Why would the date set off alarm bells in his consciousness?

Just then the bus arrived. And Rockson, with some trepidation, got in the queue and climbed aboard.

The bus was crowded, but Rockson took the seat of a man who got off at the next stop. He still felt a bit odd. He needed to sit. He absent-mindedly stared out the window as the bus cruised past block after block of new housing. Then suddenly they were in an old neighborhood of three-story brownstones and small apartment buildings. There were signs plastered on the buildings: ON THIS SITE WILL BE ERECTED EXCELLO CONDOS, LUXURY LIVING FOR THE WELL-TO-DO. Another sign said, TO BE ERECTED HERE, SENSATIONAL 105-STORY CHESSMAN CONDOS. In small print the sign continued, *Removal of the undesirables being carried out under Edict #457.*

The traffic was heavy; the bus crawled along. Rockson watched a building in the middle of the second block being entered by a group of ten or twelve red-clad rookies. They had their weed-burner nozzles in their hands, ready for action. In a short while there were screams. Windows were smashed open, flames and smoke shot out of them. More screams. Burning men and women came racing out the front door of the apartment building, followed by rookies, who were playing their flame-spouting weapons on the escapees.

Rockson was aghast. A man who was sitting next

to him said "That's the way to clear 'em out, right, citizen?"

Rockson couldn't get his eyes off the scene of carnage. He watched a mother with babe in arms crumple, her body afire, on the sidewalk. Then the bus picked up speed, and rounded a turn. *"Nietzsche Square,"* Rockson's stop was announced. He got off and was carried along in the surge of people, whisked through a tall building's doors. Kim had said he would know where his office was, but he didn't recognize this black marble lobby.

Rockson was at a loss. Then a female voice called out to him. "Ted!" A waving arm appeared over the heads of the crowd in the lobby, and within moments a red-headed woman squeezed her way through to Rockson. To his astonishment, she kissed him, long and full on his lips. She was an Amazon of a woman, big, buxom, and gorgeous.

She had greeted him like a long-lost lover. "Ted, darling, don't you have a hug for Rona?"

Rona? This is getting to be too much, thought Rockson. He recovered from his astonishment and pecked her on the forehead. She pouted, then said, "I suppose that's proper. This *is* public." She tugged on his arm. "Aren't you coming up to the office?"

Ah, a co-worker. "Sure," he said, and he was springing after her. He felt like an actor on stage. Everyone but him knew the lines, and he had to ad-lib his way through the play.

They rode up to the twentieth floor in a crowded elevator, Rona expressing her delight that Rockson was back from his "rest," and delivering office gossip and trivia—all of which meant nothing to him. When they got off, Rona pulled him to the side, behind a potted tree, and whispered in his ear.

"Ted, dearest, everyone in the office knows the *real* reason why you haven't been at work. I know Kim tried to cover up for appearances, but really, darling, these things *do* get around!" She smiled conspiratorially. "But don't worry—everyone will act as though you *were* home for a rest. So don't say anything—just act normal."

Whatever the hell "normal" is, thought Rockson.

"And, Ted?"

"Yes?"

"I'm *so* glad you're well. I was worried about you! Are we still seeing each other tonight?"

"Seeing each other?"

"Yes, darling Ted, dear. We've had the same night out every week for the past two years. Have you forgotten?"

"I—"

Rona fixed him with a stern look. "Your wife didn't make you quit the C.P.A. Bowling League, did she? It's been a perfect cover for our little rendezvous."

"Well . . ."

"I suppose she told you to skip the bowling tonight and come straight home, because of your arrest. Is that it?"

Rockson nodded, relieved.

Rona looked upset. "Really, Ted, this can't go on! You *know* how I hate being the Other Woman—" She broke off as the elevator opened again, disgorging more office workers. "Oh, hello, Fred," she said to a balding man whose pale complexion made him look

74

like he'd been in a crypt for the past ten years. "Look who's back—Mr. Rockman!" Laughing, Rona hooked her arm through Rockson's and propelled him past two huge wooden doors into an open office area.

Inside were two dozen employees who stopped what they were doing and stared at him. After an uncomfortable moment of silence, someone murmured that he should take it easy, and others joined in.

Rona took him to a door with his alter ego's name on it—Theodore Rockman—and shoved him inside. "Let me know if you need anything!" she chirped, and sailed off.

The office was much more comfortably appointed than the Rockman apartment—a sofa, large wooden desk, and potted plants. The profits of the company evidently were good, and his job rated a private office. He threw the briefcase down on the sofa.

Two walls were floor-to-ceiling windows. Rockson walked to them and looked out over the city sparkling in the sun and dry desert air. Tall buildings rose everywhere he looked.

He had scarcely been in his office two minutes when Rona reappeared and shut the door behind her. She flung herself at Rockson, wrapping her arms around his neck and smothering him with kisses. "Ted, darling, darling! You gorgeous hunk of a man! Let's do it now. Lock the door!"

This Rona sure felt terrific, and she looked fine. Rockson would have been happy to let her ravish him, except this sort of conduct undoubtedly fell on the forbidden list, which translated—once again—to the police.

He disengaged himself from her impassioned embrace. "Rona, please. Remember yourself!"

With a moan of disappointment, Rona pulled away and smoothed her hair. "I'm sorry, Ted. I couldn't help myself. You drive me wild, and if I can't see you tonight . . ." Her voice trailed off. "But you're right," she added. "This is not the proper place." She stepped up to him and wiped his cheek and lips. "You've got lipstick all over you."

Rona rearranged her clothing and left, closing the door.

Rockson dragged his sleeve across his face and ran his fingers through his mussed hair. I've got to stay here until lunch, he thought. Rock pushed paper around for three hours.

Lunchtime! He flung open his door and stalked out of the office. Rona was seated at a small desk just outside, reapplying hot-pink lipstick while she looked into a compact mirror. Evidently she was his personal secretary.

She looked up in surprise as he hurried past her. "Mr. Rockman! Where are you going?"

Rockson halted as he realized all activity in the office had stopped again, as attention was focused on him. "I—I forgot to tell you—I have to discuss a condominium purchase with a real estate man . . ."

"Oh," Rona said. "Okay, I'll see you later." He zoomed out through the big double doors and into the elevator, which was just closing its door.

Back on the street, Rockson gave an immense sigh of relief. He had to have time to put himself together. For one afternoon, at least, they could do without him. He wasn't handling his job very well anyway.

The irritating music still played everywhere, in the streets and in every vehicle and building. As he glanced around, he noticed that by and large, the people in this city seemed very—*subdued*. A little animation here and there, but most seemed to be in a zombie state much of the time, with robotlike movements and glassy eyes. Was he hallucinating? Was it some sort of paranoia, a mental breakdown?

Rockson slowed himself down and put a goofy smile on his face. Best to look like one of the crowd.

He ambled down the street, doing his best to look like a typical citizen. He was disconcerted to find people staring at him as though he had a growth on his head. He stopped and checked his reflection in a window, and saw what it was that was drawing so much attention—he still had a big pink smack on his left cheek. He carefully wiped it off.

Rookies, their uniforms bearing chess symbols, were everywhere in the city, directing traffic, strolling the sidewalks. Their presence seemed threatening to him. And why not? He was feeling and acting like a psycho.

The store windows displayed bizarre goods—more plastic things. Rockson passed cafes and restaurants. He remembered the eight dollars in his pocket—but still had no appetite.

Nearly everyone he passed was neatly dressed. The city itself had a sterilized look. So Rockson was surprised when he saw dirty derelicts loitering on street corners and sleeping in building nooks. If this society was so concerned about proper behavior and attitudes, why were these homeless and jobless not aided and taken care of? *No! Wrong!* Why were they tolerated and allowed to sully the landscape? *That* was the correct thought. His mind flip-flopped.

The TV ads said, Don't feed the homeless, let them work, the lazy bastards. *But there weren't any jobs.* Confusion.

Rockson turned a corner and came upon a man in rags pawing through a waste container, picking out scraps of food and stuffing them in his mouth. He found himself going up to the man, offering him his eight dollars, and pointing to a cafe across the street.

The derelict shook his head vehemently. "I wouldn't eat there—drugged food. All the fresh food's drugged."

Rockson was taken aback, but he pressed the man. "Eat somewhere else—anywhere you want. You don't have to go through garbage to get a meal."

The derelict moved off, shaking his head, leaving Rockson with his outstretched hand full of money. I am crazy to do this, thought Rockson. There's a law against helping these people, though I can't imagine why.

Crisscrossing, contradictory ideas filled his mind.

He continued on his way. His walk took him past a beautiful green park. He was startled when a lump in the bushes near the sidewalk moved and hissed, "Hey, you!"

He stopped and looked closely. The lump moved again and separated from the bushes—it was another derelict, a short, rotund man with several days' growth of beard and greasy clothing. Judging from his girth, he had no trouble staying fed. There was something piratelike about the man.

The man crooked a finger at him, and Rockson responded, going closer. "I've been watching you, mister—you don't look like the rest of the fine citizens of Salt Lake City."

Rockson caught his breath. Was the bum going to turn him back over to the police? He didn't answer.

The man went on. "Good for you." Rockson expelled his breath in relief. "I don't know how you managed, but you seem to be a *free* man," the derelict said, twisting his head.

"What do you mean?" Rockson said nervously.

"You *know* what I mean. Shhh! We must be careful. The police are all around, and they *listen*." The derelict peered around him with wide eyes. He crouched lower. "They'll find you out before long. Free men never last without help. But *we* can help."

"Who's 'we?' What help are you talking about?"

"Never mind. If you want help, come back to this area at night. I sleep on the grates. The name is Barrelman." With those words, the derelict drew back into the shrubbery and disappeared from sight.

"Wait!" called Rockson, but the man was gone.

Rockson was intrigued and confused at the same time.

Rock walked and walked, trying to get his mind on some definite track—and failed.

Chapter 7

Night was falling. He just *couldn't* go home. Not until he'd sorted things out. The pain in his head was getting greater by the minute. He wandered for hours, found himself in a sleazy part of town. There were more street people, darker corners, garbage. Rockson saw a red blinking neon sign; TERMINAL HOTEL—*Cheap Rooms*.

He fished in his pocket for the lunch money Kim had given him—eight bucks. He wandered into the foul-smelling lobby of the hotel. A man at the desk looked up, sized him, shrugged. "Nothing fancy—four dollars for the night. Check-out is eight A.M. Don't miss it, or you pay full day extra."

Rockson fished up the four bucks and went upstairs with the room key the man tossed him. The room was alongside the neon sign, and even with the dark shade down, the blinking leaked in. He sat down heavily on the bed. At least here, the music wasn't very loud. The buzz of the neon light also tended to blot it out.

His head hurt less. He lay down feeling less confused than when he had left work. It was the first time he was away from the music that everybody loved. He fell asleep.

There was a noise. *Scratch-Scratch.*

He awoke, sat bolt upright in bed. Raised the blind. It was still dark out—maybe after midnight. Yeah, the cheap alarm clock on the dresser said 12:10. The scratching that had awakened him was a note coming under his door.

He went over and picked it up, opened the door a crack, but saw no one in the hall. Rockson closed the door, unfolded the note.

If you need something, read the scrawl, *knock on Room 6, Stella. Before 3 a.m.*

Need something? Oh, a prostitute. Suddenly he remembered Kim and groaned. She'd be missing him. What the hell was he doing here? Then he went into the little john, turned on the faucets, and threw water in his face. He looked at his face in the cracked mirror, his white-streaked hair, his mismatched dark and light blue eyes, and thought, Who am I? *Who the hell am I?*

And dimly, a voice deep inside issued, *Doomsday Warrior. Doomsday Warrior.*

He closed his eyes, squeezed them till he saw stars. *What the hell is a Doomsday Warrior?* He couldn't remember.

"Stella—maybe Stella knows," he mumbled. "Maybe I'm here in this cheap hotel for some reason—to meet someone who knows . . ." He put on his shirt and shoes and went down the corridor to number six and knocked. A frowzy redhead in a black slip, about forty years of age, a cigarette dangling from her slash-of-red lips, opened the door.

"Yeah? Oh, you're room three? Come in, buddy. Say, you're not bad, you know. It's ten bucks extra for special things." She sat down on the bed and started pulling the slip over her head.

"I only have four bucks."

She laughed. "Down on your luck? Well, so am I, so am I. . . . Tell you what, Mister Number Three, I'll make you a deal: I get to keep all the money I find in your pockets, and that will be the charge. Okay?"

She was disappointed to find that he told the truth, but said, "A deal's a deal."

Before he knew what was happening, she was stripped. Naked. She was well-built, bony, hard eyed. He felt the urge—primitive, unbridled. He mounted her.

"Never had a man like you," she said afterward. She lit a cigarette with shaky hands. "You're great! Where you from? Out of town?"

"Out of town," he mumbled.

"Thought so," she said, "Nothin' like you around *here*. Say, you got a job or something? You want to live with me?"

"No . . . got a wife," he said. "Got a wife."

"Don't they *all*," Stella said, sliding her black rayon slip back over her tight body. "How about every Tuesday and Thursday, after work? Only ten bucks— Hell, that's reasonable."

"Ten bucks," he muttered. "Sounds . . . okay . . ."

"Then, it's settled, honey." She came over and kissed him. "Say, can you stay out all night tonight?"

"No," he said. "Got to go home, home . . ."

"Well, you come back tomorrow—Mr. . . . What's your name?"

"Ted."

"Well, see you tomorrow midnight, here, Mr. Ted."

He went back to his room and stared into the mirror. God, he was hungry, and the cheap whiskey he had swallowed in the redhead's room was clawing at his gut. His pupils were like pinholes.

He felt like he had betrayed his wife. He felt ashamed. He had wanted to ask Stella—something. And instead he'd had sex with her! He had to throw up.

Rockson went to the sink, vomited repeatedly, then he sunk down to the tile floor. He sobbed down on his hands and knees. They'd take him away now—they'd put him in the city dump . . .

He stood up. He saw his wild-eyed countenance in the mirror over the sink. He yelled *"You!* You are a sinner!" He smashed his right fist into the image. The glass shattered.

It hurt. His hand was bleeding.

Bleeding . . . *Blood* . . . Bloodfruit.

Bloodfruit! He remembered now. Remembered the desert and the Russians *and* the storm!

The timestorm! The *Kala-Ka*! The time-tornado!

"Doomsday Warrior," he muttered, *"I'm* the Doomsday Warrior! I *am* Rockson, a Freefighter, I was in a desert—the Reds had dragged me—the KGB officer, his name is Streltsy, he . . ." It all flooded back to him. He *knew* now. He was exultant. The headache had gone away. He knew who he was. The sex, the hunger, the drinks, the painful bleeding hand, had cleared his mind. He didn't know what was

83

going on, yet. But he knew who he was! He didn't want his identity to slip away. He kept shouting: "I am the Doomsday Warrior, a Freefighter. It's 2092 A.D. I fight the Russians! They nuked America! I am the Doomsday Warrior!"

There was a banging on the door. "Hey, mac, I don't care *who* the hell you think you are! Quit it, it's two A.M. Some of the people in this fleabag hotel have to get up in the morning!"

He shut up. He put on his jacket and coat and left by the front stairs, throwing the key on the counter. The clerk shrugged. "No refund."

He wandered toward what he hoped was Archer Street and the bus that would take him home. That's what he would do now. He'd go home, explain to Kim who he *really* was. Maybe his wife could tell him what the hell the joke was, what the hell the world was pulling on him. And she would help him leave this place.

He stopped in his tracks—No, she wouldn't. She'd call the police. The police—rookies—would put him in that cell again, play him the loud music again, and he would forget who he was. In the dark, sodden streets he walked on.

Clang-bing-Bang . . . "Yeow!" The sudden racket activated Rockson's lightning reflexes. He spun full around, his powerful arms snapping into defensive positions, legs poised like sprung steel, senses bristling . . . He confronted . . . a rangy pole-thin alley cat examining the contents of an overturned garbage can.

"Meow," the cat said, half frightened, half amused.

"Why, you little . . ." Rockson chuckled. "You damn well scared the livin' bejesus outta me, you little rodent."

"Meow," the bold tomcat protested, indicating he was only trying to make an honest living.

"All right, all right. Just don't sneak up on me like that, will ya, please?"

Rockson turned back to the long stretch of potholed street running down a slight incline along the city's backside. A misty rain added a veneer of gloss to the dismal scene. The scene was lit by a lone streetlight, and an occasional whisp of moonlight from behind low black clouds highlighted a few of the street's features: a battered Cadillac resting on cement blocks, stripped bare to the body . . . a faded COLD STORAGE sign over a warehouse's rusted gate . . . a fish house, its windows long boarded over . . . a dead neon script that identified the entrance to the defunct Mill Street Union Hall.

Far ahead, maybe a mile, mile and a half down the incline of the street, a blinking red light beaconed. Darkness consumed the remaining stretches of the neglected, patchwork roadway. It was a street with more of a past than a future. Rock proceeded cautiously along the rows of low-level, indecorous warehouses and abandoned garages that flanked the street, encroaching the low curb that allowed a brief walk on either side. He straightened himself and took a deep breath.

"Ted Rockson, C.P.A.," he said on reaching the streetlight and catching sight of his reflection in a shop window. The wooly suit itched like a rug and he squirmed around inside it, his broad shoulders stretching the material, his slender hips floating in it. Setting down the briefcase he carried, he adjusted his collar and tie, stretching his powerful neck to ease the strain on the button and centering the broad, checkered tie. He had to chuckle at the sight of himself in the dusty window, reflected against a disheveled collection of plumbing fixtures.

Rockson marveled at the ridiculous nature of the clothing he had been forced to don to pass as a "respected citizen." Cumbersome, ostentatious, and impractical, it seemed to hinder movement rather than encourage it. And the necktie! What could the purpose be except to cut off the flow of blood to the brain! Incredible. Simply incredible.

He had turned to pick up the jaunty briefcase, when he noticed a pair of feet sticking out from underneath the front end of an auto in front of him. Steeled to fight, he glided into position and grabbed the shoeless appendages, pulling forward with a quick jerk. They were attached to a young black-haired boy with a hint of a mustache and a cigarette dangling from his lips, patches of grease covering those portions of his face not consumed with pimples. He was on his back on a mechanic's floor caddy, and rolled easily into the street from underneath the jacked-up Chrysler.

"I'm not stealing anything. Honest, mister. It's my car. I swear!" the wide-eyed boy protested, a wrench in one hand, the car's recently amputated starter in the other.

"It's okay," Rock began. "I know there's no jobs and you have to—"

Evidently the boy feared the worse from the "solid citizen," and kicked his legs free. First the wrench, then the starter, came flying at Rockson's head. He bobbed and dodged the missiles. The nimble youth was in flight, streaking back up the street.

Rockson had no sooner opened his mouth to call the kid back when a blinding light, like a hundred orange-red flashbulbs set off at once, burst the darkness, engulfing the fleeing youth.

"Eeeeeyeaaaaaaaah!" the midnight-mechanic screeched in agony, still running, his clothes and skin afire from head to toe. He ran and tumbled a good twenty yards, bellowing in gut-wrenching pain as the flames reduced him to a smoldering mound of charred flesh and fiber.

A weed-burner! Where?

Rockson froze, shocked but alert, twitching as a rush of adrenaline surged through his body. The clip-clop of heavy boots on the pavement announced the approach of the boy's murderer. A giant of a man emerged from the shadows into the shaft of light cast by the streetlamp. The uniformed stranger approached slowly, confidently, in measured steps, his visage hidden behind a mirror-faced visor. He carried a rodlike weapon attached by a hose to a small tank which hung on his back.

"Homeless bastard," the man said, turning the nozzle of his weapon and affixing it to a clip on his belt next to a long metal nightstick.

Rockson took stock of his opponent. The man's bulky, muscular frame filled his sleek nylon uniform with the distinctive rook patch over his heart. Besides the torch weapon and the nightstick, a long killing knife hung from his wide leather belt.

"Yeah . . ." answered Rockson with a forced grin. His disguise was working. He wanted to avoid trouble for now. It was too late for the kid anyway. Still, Rock wanted to *kill*.

The rook stopped short about ten feet from Rockson and turned to look at the smoldering mess in the roadway. They both watched as the flames flickered in the midst of rain that continued to drift across the scene.

"Did he give you any trouble . . . citizen?" the rook asked Rockson, still looking away from him.

"You got the bastard first, officer. Why, he just bolted out from nowhere all of a sudden—homeless bastard. Pain in the ass. They're everywhere, aren't they?"

"Are they?" said the rook, turning back toward Rockson, taking three short steps forward, toward the middle of the street.

Rockson backed into the car, stumbling on the mechanic's floor caddy, trying to appear clumsy and frightened.

"Well, I, ah, mean . . . there's far too many of them . . ." Rockson was having trouble controlling his anger at the cop. But he did.

"One less now, I'd say," said the rook, looking back again with satisfaction at the remains.

"Yes yes, excellent job. Commendable. I must notify your superiors. Thank you, officer . . ." He smiled wanly.

"Well, it's late—isn't it? Guess I'll be on my way. Good evening, officer."

"On your way . . . *where*?" demanded the rook,

taking three more quick steps to head off Rockson's retreat.

"Where? Why, er . . . Home, of course. Where every good citizen should be. In the bosom of my family."

"And just where is your, ah, home?"

"Southeast Tenth Street." Rockson said, sensing the game was up.

"Southeast Tenth? Why, you must know Captain Black. He lives on the one-hundred block." Rockson wondered if the comment were a trap.

"Captain Black? Well, I, ah, I don't get out much I'm afraid. Much too busy. I'm a C.P.A., you know. Work work work. Busy as a bee. You understand."

"Of course. And just what firm are you affiliated with, may I ask . . . citizen?" He played with the nozzle on his belt.

"What firm?" Rockson didn't know. "I'm an independent. Took over Dad's firm, you know," he improvised.

"An independent, are you? Admirable. *Admirable.* Not many independents left these days. I didn't catch the name, citizen."

"Rockman. Theodore Rockman . . . officer."

"And you wouldn't mind showing me your papers. Just a formality, of course. One can't be too careful in these troubled times."

"My papers?" Oh no . . . no problem, officer. Of course," said Rockson, fumbling through his pockets. He'd left them at the hotel, in Stella's room. Damn it! "Why . . . heh heh, yes. How embarrassing. It seems I've left my papers behind. How silly of me."

The rookie reached for his nightstick, said, "I think

I'll knock some sense into you, *homeless*, before I *burn you*!"

"I'm not homeless, I'm the fucking Doomsday Warrior!" With that shout, Rockson's foot found the handy-dandy mechanic's dolly and sent it slamming into the rookie's shins, bringing the hefty cop reaching down in pain. The Doomsday Warrior was ripe for a fight and came up with a solid karate kick to the neck, only to have his foot crack against the heavy plastic visor protecting his adversary's face. The blow did succeed in jerking the man upright, and Rockson, quickly shaking off the pain in his foot, hopped onto the dolly. Using it like a skateboard, he slammed his shoulder into the man's gut, forcing an *umph* from him as the wind left his body.

But Rock had engaged a worthy opponent. The young giant of a man was in excellent shape, and by his movements a martial-arts expert himself. Rockson stood him up with three dead shots to the neck and chest, but with the man's face protected by the visor, Rockson was unable to get the haymaker in. So, mustering himself into a coil and unleashing a vicious spinning kick dead center of the visor, Rockson succeeded in splitting the thick plastic. The shattered helmet flew in two directions, revealing the giant's massive cranium. A huge smile crossed the rook's grim visage exposing a row of teeth the size of bottlecaps, a broad rumpled forehead with heavy black eyebrows overhanging close-set beady eyes, and receding hairline backed by short-cropped reddish hair. The man reminded Rockson of a Russian he had tangled with somewhere . . . somehow . . .

"I knew you was a homeless bastard, you termite.

Just like that other grease spot I fried up. So, you wanna play rough, do ya? Heh heh."

Whoosh. His massive arm reached out in a powerful swipe with the metal nightstick, Rockson just ducking under its fatal path.

Whoosh, the nightstick returned, lower, forcing Rockson to jump high in the air, the behemoth advancing step after step, controlling the offensive now.

"Solid citizen, hey?"

Swoosh.

"Took over Dad's firm, hey?"

Swoosh.

Enough, thought Rockson, prepared for the next blow. It came just as he had anticipated. The Doomsday Warrior grabbed the rookie's arm as he struck, pulling him forward with his own momentum and deftly lifting the long killing knife from its sheath on the belt, ending up behind his opponent. Before the mighty but outmatched rook could recover, the Rock had succeeded in slicing through the man's heavy boot and cutting into his Achilles tendon on the right leg, crippling him instantly.

The rook wasn't laughing anymore. This was no helpless vagrant or defenseless teenager he was bullying now. This dude was *tough*! He sprang like a lynx, had the strength of a bear, and the cunning of a fox. Tossing the useless nightstick aside, he reached for his flamethrower and ignited it. Rockson leapt sideways from a wall of flames while the rook fumbled to turn on his helmet radio and send for help.

"Code nine . . . Section eight. Code nine . . . section eight . . ." he shrieked into the radio. "Send

91

back up. *Hurry!* Do you read me!"

Rockson flipped the knife from hand to hand as the rook backed him against the wall of the building with his twenty-foot flames. The sound of closing sirens cut through the foggy night air. Soon he'd be corralled by a whole gaggle of these goons.

Rock spotted an opening. Flicking the knife with blinding speed he sent it sailing. It skimmed the rook's neck and severed the hose feeding his torch. Instantly the pressurized gel ignited, engulfing the beefy tough guy in sticky hellfire. Screaming and rotating, beating at his body, he fell.

"That's for the kid," Rockson snarled. In one long bound, he leaped upward, catching hold of the COLD STORAGE sign, then climbed from window to window, reaching the roof of the warehouse. He stopped long enough to watch a gang of howling, flashing squad cars race onto the street from both directions.

Darting across the roof, he took a fire escape down to an alleyway behind the building. And walked on, unhurried, like nothing had ever happened. He turned a corner, nearly bumping into a figure. He grabbed the man. His pathetic yell was stifled by Rock's hand over his mouth. Rockson stared into the man's eyes. Middle-aged, dressed in topcoat, alcohol on his breath. "If I let go of your mouth, don't scream."

The man nodded.

Rockson let up on his grip. The man trembled. "Please — take my money — my wallet."

"I don't want your money," the Doomsday Warrior snarled. "I want answers."

"Answers?"

"Yeah. Who runs this town? What is this place?"

"What?" the man's eyes widened.

"You heard me!" Rock grabbed him by the collar, lifted him off the ground. "Who runs this crummy town?"

The man was pale as a sheet. "Chessman! Chessman runs this town, everyone knows that!"

"Where is he? Where do I find this Chessman?"

"In — in the Tabernacle. Oh my god, you're crazy! A psycho! You're going to kill me, aren't you?" A foam of fear drooled from his lips. Suddenly he gasped, clutched his chest, slumped.

Rockson dropped the man, "No," he said as he walked away in the downpour, "*I'm* not killing you. Fear did it."

He knew *who* he was, and now the Doomsday Warrior knew *where* he had to go for the answers — to the Tabernacle. He'd find this Chessman and wring the truth from him about this hideous, sick game he was playing!

Chapter 8

Rockson, with gathering determination, walked on. He came to a better part of town. The digital clock on a billboard flashed *4 A.M. Temp 39 degrees*. Cold. In the murky mist ahead at the end of the park was the tall gothic Tabernacle—the Tabernacle that he knew from his history lessons had been destroyed—along with Salt Lake City and most other cities in America—on September 11th, 1989. The Reds had dropped hundreds of ICBMs on an unsuspecting America on that date.

A newspaper lay on one of the benches of a small park Rockson passed. He picked it up. September 8, 1989. Headline: PEACE TALKS HIT A SNAG.

Yeah, they sure did, he thought. A *real* snag. But if this was the past, there was something wrong about it. The police were wrong, for one thing. He knew from his history books that the city was wrong too. This place was some sort of *alternate* past. An alternate past that the time-tornado had taken him to. But assuming the war happened here too, it was just three days to Armageddon. Would it happen? Or could the past change?

It was all useless speculation at this point. There was no way to check his guesswork, no brilliant Dr. Schecter to sit down and have a cup of coffee with and ruminate about space-time. No Glowers, those ancient, all-wise beings of the radioactive western deserts of his own space-time, to consult. No, he was here in Salt Lake City in 1989, and he had to make his move.

"Hey, you there . . . Stop!"

Oh, not again, thought Rockson.

As the rookie swung his nightstick, Rockson grabbed the man's wrist. *This* rookie had a knife in his belt too. He reached for the knife with his left hand. But the huge bowie-like blade of the rookie was slowly turned by the superior power of the Doomsday Warrior. It plunged deep into his red-shirted gut. The rookie slid down to the wet ground.

Rockson wiped the knife on the rookie's sleeve and slipped it into his waistband. He knew he should get away from here. Two bodies—a block apart!

A flashing blue neon light beckoned to him. BAR . . . BAR . . . BAR, it offered. He started moving. He turned toward the sign, away from the more-brightly-lit street. He could hear the music, soft but insistent, coming from a lightpole here. There were speakers on *all* the lightpoles. Darkness seemed to mean no speakers, no music. The speakers were connected to the lights.

The music. He snapped his fingers—*that's it*! He remembered who he was when he first came into the city. But after exposure to the music—particularly in the Loud Room at the police station—those terrible headaches began. Then, when Kim came to get him,

95

he was somehow convinced that he belonged to this horrible city. But he *didn't*. The music had brainwashed him into forgetfulness, complacency.

But he'd be complacent no more. The nuke war *would* come in just days, and now he had to act! He'd try to escape with as many of the poor inhabitants of this dizzy burg as possible before the bombs fell. But none of the brainwashed citizens would believe or follow him. Kim and the kids wouldn't even understand—unless he could shut off the power of the Chessman: the hypno-music that was broadcast twenty-four hours a day. The music that couldn't be stopped.

That must be his first objective! Destroy the radio-broadcast center—wherever it was. He'd find it—and Chessman—for he was the Doomsday Warrior, the Ultimate American!

He approached the tavern, pushed the swinging door to the bar open.

He walked to the counter. A waiter wiping a glass asked, "What'll you have, mac?"

Rockson thought for a second. If this is really 1989, there's supposed to be a terrific drink . . . He remembered the name.

"Jack Daniel's, neat," he said.

The bartender chuckled. "Don't make me laugh, citizen. You know we don't carry the good stuff—but you want whiskey, we got."

He poured out a shot glass for Rockson. He drank it. It was like fire in his throat. He motioned for a glass of water. The bartender chuckled again and slid one down the counter. Another customer—the only one—a dark, swarthy man, hunched over in an overcoat, collar up and hat down, sat at the other end of the bar.

He looked over at Rockson. He smiled. He stood from his stool, sauntered over, "Buddy, can I buy you a drink?"

Rockson, realizing he had no money, nodded. The man sat beside him. "Out late, huh?"

Rockson's eyes narrowed. "What's it to you?"

"No offense. I'm out late too. The missus."

Rockson relaxed, took the refilled glass. "Down the hatch." The second shot burned less.

The man smiled, "I thought so! Your missus threw you out, too, right?" The bartender moved away, bored.

"Something like that," Rock said tersely.

The man offered his hand. "My name is Lang. I'm a fitter. What's your name and occupation, citizen?"

"Rockman, C.P.A." Rock said, duplicating the way the man identified himself, so as not to seem a stranger hereabouts.

"C.P.A., huh?" He smiled, "Here's to accounts."

"Yeah," said Rock. "To settling accounts."

The music drifting over the speakers in the street started to annoy him now—he wanted to drown it out. He looked around the barroom, and his eyes alighted on something ancient and wonderful. "Hey, a *jukebox*—got some good songs in there, bartender?"

"Plug's out," said the bartender. "Has been since the coup d' état."

"What coup d' état?"

"Boy, are you loaded," said Lang. "Why, the one that put the honorable Chessman in over ten years

97

ago. Everyone knows the story. Every citizen had to take a course in the glory of the coup."

"Well, *tell* the story, citizen," Rock sneered. "I need a recap, or I might get a little crazy, you know?" He narrowed his eyes and tried to look crazy, which wasn't hard after all he'd been through. "I'm listening."

"Okay, *okay*," said the customer, "No—no need to get hostile, citizen. It goes like this. Once upon a time the city was a mess and there was this here chessmasters' convention here, *sec*, a great gathering. There were Russians and all sorts of people competing, but the chessman was the best—he won. Anyway, the chess contestants met at night and talked about what a big mess the city was in and vowed to do something about it. There was bad music everywhere and kids running amok, and no honor among husbands and wives, and lots of disorder, and there was no *Twenty Questions* quiz program on TV even—imagine that!"

"Imagine that," Rock said. "Go on!"

"Well, then, there were only two contestants. Chessman was one."

"What's the Chessman's name?" The bartender came back down the polished mahogany. "Easy, mac. The Chessman is just the Chessman. His opponent, the American, cheated. Chessman shot him down as he deserved. When the cops came to arrest the righteous and innocent Chessman, his folks pulled their Uzis and offed the pigs, you see? Now lower your voice, or leave."

"In a minute. Tell me the rest, Lang," Rock demanded.

"Ch-Chessman's men went to city hall and shot the

politicians, and so *that* was the coup d' état—except they had to shoot a lot of people in the Tabernacle too, to take it over."

"Didn't the city call out the U.S. Army or something to stop Chessman?" Rockson tried to look as if he were measuring Lang for a coffin.

"No—n-no! Everyone was sick of the disorder." He licked dry lips.. "The Chessman replaced the cops with the rookies. He lives in the Tabernacle and now his sweet muzik is broadcast from there, and there's social order and progress for everyman, and nobody has to worry their heads about elections or who's right or wrong—the chessman tells us. Simple, isn't it?"

"Very simple." Rock frowned. A brainwashed city in the control of a dictator that has everyone in his thrall.

"Tell me about the police."

The bartender squinted. "Tell him, then out he goes!"

"The Chessman is commander in chief of all the red police forces. The old blueshirt police are gone. Chessman replaced the police hierarchy with the consultants. We call them the thought police. They have trank-wands that can tranquilize for one half-hour. The—the consultants started out as chess advisers. Chessman, once he took over, gradually used them to replace the civil servants on the highest level. Particularly the police commissioner and the precinct captains. He rightfully didn't trust them.

"He replaced the patrol cops with rookies armed with submachine guns. Their cars can't go down the twisting narrow streets, so the Chessman has the red

99

knights. They're on horseback and can travel down alleys and walkways. Originally, they were park maintenance workers and they had small weed-burners to kill weeds. Their weed-burners grew to flamethrower size, because the homeless are such a threat nowadays.

"You must have seen the big police trucks. They were originally litter pickers for the Parks Department. Now their small litter collectors are huge twenty-five-ton 'Brush-eaters,' sometimes used to clear fallen branches and overgrowth. But because of the emergency, they have special powers. Daring and diligent, they go after the homeless, chew 'em up — mostly late at night. They are the front line against the derelicts."

Rockson wanted to know more. "How about the music? How come there's only one kind of music?"

"Only muzik is allowed now. M-U-Z-I-K, not music," he spelled it out. It's nice, not like rock and roll."

"Time's up, mac. Get out. Leave my customer alone!" snarled the bartender. Rockson snickered. "Not likely, mac. I want the jukebox plugged in."

The bartender started objecting, but then Rockson pulled out the knife. "I *said*, I want to play the juke." In a flash, the cowed bartender handed Rockson four quarters. "Here, it won't play anything without money. Plug's on the right."

After telling the men to keep their hands visible, Rockson went over, plugged the machine in, checked out the selections.

Barry Manilow? He'd never heard of that one. Let's see, from the archival tapes of Century City he remembered the names of some of the *greats*. Maybe there would be one here — an old song he could trust to not be programming his mind. Jefferson Starship? No, that didn't ring a bell. Oh, here's one: "Johnny B. Good", by Chuck Berry. He put the quarters in the slot and the dusty needle dropped onto B3.

The sound was loud and clean and refreshing. "*Way back up in the woods way down near New Orleans . . .* "

Rockson's shoulders relaxed visibly. He realized they had been hunched in an almost-cringing response to the muzik pouring out of the lightpoles and ceiling speakers for the past few days.

He hit four more selections he remembered from the Century City archives: "Eight Miles High," by the Byrds, "Satisfaction," by the Rolling Stones, and a song each by Hank Williams and Loretta Lynn. The Stones came on first, hot and loud. What a relief! The two cowards still had their hands on the bar as he had ordered. They had beads of sweat crawling down their foreheads. They eyed Rockson nervously. "Another whiskey," Rock said. He noticed that when the bartender went to pour, he picked up a different bottle. Rock smiled.

"If you're trying to give me a Mickey Finn," he said, "Forget it. I'm from the future. I'm the Doomsday Warrior, a mutant Freefighter. I'm immune to most poisons and sedatives."

The barman said, "Anything you say, mister! *Sure*, you're — you're from the future. I got no problem with that, mac. I believe you." Now he started shaking, but he put down the bottle and poured from the original one. He seemed really terrified. "Say, look, why don't you take what's in the register and leave. Nobody will

101

call the cops, you just—"

"Shut up and pour," Rockson insisted.

The bartender did, spilling half the drink in the process. While Rockson downed the whiskey, Lang cut for the door. He was out in a flash. Rock heard him yelling, "Help! A madman's in the bar, help, he's got a knife!"

Rockson shoved the bartender away and tore out into the street. He could hear the rookies' whistles now—the sound of sirens too in the distance. The first glow of the red morning sun was creeping up on the tall glass skyscrapers. He'd have to run for it. He needed a weapon—a good one. Damn it. Why hadn't he taken along that rookie's pistol?

He ran down one street, then another—what's that? A giant plastic revolver hanging up over a store. POLICE SUPPLIES, the sign read. *Class 5 licenses required for purchases.* Another sign stuck in the door said, *Closed for the day.* No, it *wasn't.* He smashed the door open with the heel of his shoe—a dropkick that nearly tore it off its hinges. He was inside in an instant. He closed the door. The steel shutters over the window would hide him from view. With eager eyes, he perused the glass compartments filled with every conceivable twentieth-century weapon. It was dim, but Rockson had good night vision.

Surely there must be something here he could use! Rock was a firm believer in seizing the opportunity, making the best of things at hand. He missed his super-fast and accurate Liberator weapon. But the twentieth century, after all, was the home of some exquisitely deadly arms. He'd find *something.*

Although Rockson was interested in finding as

modern a weapon as possible, his interest in guns made him stop and admire the antique gun display behind the counter. Amazing! All sorts of wild-west stuff—authentic. He found the keys to the case holding the old weapons and opened it. He took out a long-barreled revolver that Wyatt Earp would have been proud to own—a Colt Peacemaker. He knew this to be one of the first—if not *the* first—handgun to be chambered for the .45 caliber long Colt cartridge. A formidable weapon, date circa 1873. It loaded forty grains of FFg black powder with 255-grain lead bullets. The gleaming seven-and-a-half-inch barrel made it fairly accurate too, from what he remembered reading.

He spun the chamber, it moved smooth; well-oiled. He clicked the trigger. Sounded good, very good. With great reluctance he put the six-shooter down. He needed something like a three-hundred-shooter if he was going to get anywhere in this damned city.

He was hoping that there was something in the shop they kept away from all but the best customers—somewhere a hidden case of illegal firepower. Lots of these old gunshops had had a brisk trade in illegal automatic weapons.

Rock searched high and low, ignoring other fine weapons he came across, until he found a loose floorboard—and ripped it up. In a clear plastic case under the floorboards he found something heavy and black. He unzipped the case and pulled out an Uzi. And whistled. An Uzi was a completely automatic weapon manufactured in Israel and shipped to the U.S. in great numbers illegally just before World War III. It was the favorite weapon of terrorists. The Uzi made small men big, timid men brave. The Uzi was to machine guns what the Colt .45 was to revolvers. It was so dependable that the snub-snouted Uzi, even when fouled by dust and grit, functioned.

The Middle Eastern submachine gun had a fold-down stock, a "double elbow" arrangement ideal for concealment. The Uzi could be taken down to 24 inches in length. With the stock opened, it was barely 32 inches long. Yet it packed a cyclic rate of fire of three hundred rounds per minute. Rockson wished the clips held more than twenty-five rounds. Maybe he could make some modifications — find larger clips that would fit.

He snapped his fingers. This was a completely outfitted gun shop — maybe it had some manufacturing equipment in the back room, not just storage. He pushed the second door open and in the dimness saw a metal-turning lathe. Better than he could have hoped! But he'd have to have electricity. He tried the light switch, after shutting the interior door. A light came on. Luck. In a short while he had the lathe spinning, and placed the Uzi on its clamp holder. He had a lot of work ahead of him — *hours*. But he was elated. He would update the Uzi with spare parts from some of the other weapons in the front room — including some long clips from the badly damaged Browning antiair World War II vintage weapon in the window display. Still, the Browning's barrel was clean . . .

Working efficiently but rapidly, Rockson took the classic Colt .45 and a Widley .45 magnum — which could chamber 200-grain slugs — out of the cases in the front room and started disassembling them. He found some cases of 9mm bullets manufactured in Finland, too. Good ammo.

The barrel assembly of the magnum weapon consisted of a ribbed barrel, poston, and bolt housing. The other weapons weren't meant to come apart in the same way, but with Rockson's skill, they did. The lathe made a lot of noise. It couldn't be helped. In two and a half hours, using the clips meant for the Browning antiaircraft weapon that held a hundred rounds each, he finished his work. Rockson turned off the lathe, undid the clamps, and held his Uzi-Colt-Widley-Browning antiair hybrid weapon. A beauty of deadly power!

Sure it was heavy, but it was meant for heavy work — and it still could be concealed under a coat held over one arm. Damn, if this compound gun couldn't do the trick, what weapon could?

He took six of the long Browning bandoliers along. Lots of high-caliber death for any opponents. It made his clothes fit terribly, but what the hell. It paid to be well-armed more than it paid to be well-tailored.

Chapter 9

Rockson's anger knew no bounds. He'd smash this Chessman and his hypnotic power, destroy the damned police who cremated innocent people, who kept this burg under their thumb. But *how*, alone?

He remembered the derelict outside his office building. The one who had whispered for Rockson to come see him if he was really a free man. Perhaps there was an opposition to Chessman—allies.

Rock left the shop with the gun covered by his jacket held over his arm. It was a sullen wet day. He reached the dark alley near Nietzsche Square, where he'd gotten off the bus to go to work. There were the trashbins that the street person had been rummaging through. But nowhere was the decrepit man to be seen.

He went over to the little corner newsstand. "Citizen, where are the street people that used to congregate here?"

The toothless newsman smiled. "The brush-eaters got some of them. Came the other night, caught two or three. The rest runs off. They'd be back over in Sadtown, the city dump—if any are left. That's where they belong, the filthy, shiftless bastards!"

Rockson asked where Sadtown was. The newsdealer said earnestly, "Wouldn't go down there, fella—lots of street people—they eats off the dump there—should be closed down." Still, he gave the Doomsday Warrior directions.

Rockson came to the south edge of the city. The city dump. There he saw people you could hardly identify as such, scurrying and foraging around the piles of garbage with the rats. He grabbed one. "I'm looking for Barrelman—Do you know where he is?"

The man told him, "Third pile to the left," and pulled free.

Rockson made his way over the shifting piles of reeking garbage till he found Barrelman, who looked up and smiled. "You are free? Glory be. Just don't eat fresh food—it's not only the muzik, it's the food, that hypnotizes. Drink a lot of liquor—keeps your mind off of it. At night, especially when you sleep, take care—sleep up on a roof. The brush-eaters can't climb stairs well, and make a lot of noise doing it. That's my advice." He went back to picking garbage.

"Thanks for the advice," said Rockson, "but I need more than advice on survival." He pulled the coat from his arm. "See this weapon here? It can kill a hundred rookies—I want you to get the street people together to fight back. I can show you how to make these weapons. I made mine from parts at a gun store. There must be hundreds of you strong enough to fight the Chessman's tyranny. Talk to me, *damn it. Who* is Chessman?"

107

Barrelman put down a soup can. "Very well, citizen. Chessman was the Soviet chess champion, here in the city for a match," Barrelman said. "He was caught cheating—a hidden mike in his ear. He was getting help from a team of Soviet grandmasters in a hotel across the way. Chess federation threw him out of the contest, declared the American champion to be the winner. Then Chessman lead a coup . . ."

"Yeah, I heard about that—skip it. What is Chessman like? Is he strong?"

"Well, as strong as five men, they say. And he has powers of illusion, I'm told. Powers to use your own mind against you."

"Sounds like bull to me," said Rock, frowning. "He's just a man with an organization behind him, and lots of technology."

"I wouldn't be too sure, Rock. Chessman killed his queen—his wife—with mere powers of his *mind*. She was mentally forced to drink poison. He can control your mind."

"Not likely. The propaganda machine must have made his whole thing up—to keep people in fear. Without his machines and rookies and drugs, without all the fear, he's human.

"Storm the condos. Take what's yours. Be free." Barrelman looked straight into his steely eyes, then downward.

"A few hundred of us could fight. But many others are weak, sick in the head, after years of this life," muttered Barrelman. "I tell you, citizen, freedom is just a pipe dream. There was an attempt right after the coup to stop the Chessman, but it failed. The muzik speakers went up, the food was filled with tranks, and the control squares were created. We live on the edge, poor and hungry and sick. But free. We have no will to fight, though. Believe me, it's hopeless."

"A hundred men will do, Barrelman," Rock insisted. "Get them together—here—while there's still time. Why did you ask me to come see you, otherwise? What did I risk my life to seek you out for?"

Barrelman shrugged. "I wanted to have you among us—we like to see citizens fall into our ranks, that's all. We are fewer every day. We need recruits. So's we don't die out. You go and do your violent business—we can't fight. We *won't* fight. It's hopeless."

Rockson's shoulders sagged. It did seem hopeless.

"I don't belong here," Rockson said. "I must get to my home—far away. Why don't you all simply leave the city—go somewhere."

Barrelman sighed. "There isn't anything outside the city." He pointed to the far end of the garbage dump. "That mist over there—we call it the Veil—surrounds the whole city."

Rock looked where the old codger was pointing. "It just looks like a mist to me. Maybe smoke, that's all."

"Don't believe me? You can go over to it and stick your head through—but it won't let you out of the city. Try to push through and it pushes you back."

"I think I *will* try it," Rock said, and went over the garbage piles until he was nose-against the mist. He pushed his head against it—and through. He could see the desert surrounding the city now—barren, still. He pulled back, moved about fifty feet from the Veil, and ran toward it with all his might. Like a thousand gathered rubber bands, it shoved him back. He fell and rolled.

"Told you," Barrelman yelled. "Chessman won't let nobody escape the city. Controls the Veil from his Tower, he does. And no one can get in there."

Rockson felt along the Veil for some distance. It didn't have any gaps, as far as he walked—until he heard a hissing, like escaping air. He looked twenty feet further along the rolling piles of debris. And there was a strange sight. It had been hidden from his view before, when he had stood with Barrelman, by the debris. It looked like a lens shutter, purple and red, swirling. Suspended in the air.

"Hey," Barrelman yelled, "don't go near that! It's dangerous, and it ain't what you're looking for."

"What is it?" Rockson watched as Barrelman, waving frantically, approached. "It's the Portal," the old man gasped, reaching Rockson's side. "Don't mess with it. Go through it and as sure as hell you wind up downtown on the big bridge. It's *damned* dangerous, drops you in traffic! You could get run over downtown on that busy highway."

"The highway bridge?" Rock said, grabbing Barrelman. "Did you say if you go in the Portal, you wind up on the highway bridge downtown?"

"Yup."

Rockson remembered the bridge. That was where he had first appeared in this mad world—after the time-storm had sucked him into it. Maybe if *he* walked through the Portal he'd wind up back in the *future, not* on the highway bridge. It was worth a try. Excitedly, he threw Barrelman the compound gun.

"See you *later*," Rock said. He ran pell-mell toward the spinning mass. Like a sprinter bound on winning

110

first prize, he ran over the rolling piles of debris, down an incline of crushed cans and ashes, and plunged into the mist. It felt wet—like hitting a fog bank. And cold.

Rockson found himself ducking through traffic on the very same highway bridge downtown. *On the roadway!* Horns blared, brakes screeched. *God!* He avoided a car, got on the sidewalk, and sat on the curb, thinking. After a while he had another idea. Maybe if he had more speed, more *power* behind him, he'd succeed. He ran off the bridge, and down several streets until he was in a parking lot behind a tall condominium. He looked for a *good* car. He passed up several two-door economy jobs, even a big Caddy. He needed *real* speed.

He found it! A spanking-red Porsche. He smashed the driver's-side window with a rock. The alarm went off, but the wiring was simple and he cut it off quickly. The ignition system was likewise routine electrical circuitry. Rock managed to hot-wire it in a minute.

He roared off, feeling his way through the smooth gears, headed south toward the city dump. He took Highway 15, blowing his horn, taking the left lane, swinging madly around the other cars. He hit 110 mph. He remembered the ramp down to the dump had a small sign. GARBAGE RAMP. The sanitation trucks used it early in the morning.

In a matter of minutes Rock reached the ramp and swung off the road. Rockson got up some more speed on the ramp; he roared the Porsche along between the heaps of refuse, down the sandy road used by the garbage trucks. The pickers on the garbage piles,

Barrelman included, looked up in amazement as the flashy new sports car screeched down the lane, tearing up a huge cloud of dirt and cinders. A madman was driving at over a hundred miles per hour right at the Portal. And he disappeared.

Rockson was on the *same* highway bridge again. He had failed to get through to his own time. What's more, he was hurtling the Porsche directly at an oncoming red car — a rookie-filled Toyota Camry. He started to hit the brakes and then he saw the eyes of the frantic driver. He was about to chicken out, and Rockson *wasn't*. The rookie car swerved, jumped the curb, and tore through the railing. It sailed out far into the air before it nosed over and fell the three hundred or so feet to the pavement below.

Rockson brought the Porsche under control.

He pulled over. Traffic was light, and only an occasional car passed him by as he sat there thinking. Then it as if a light bulb had lit up in his head. He realized that he hadn't come *out* of the future in the dump, so why should he expect to go *into* the future that way. The Portal wasn't the time-door, *this bridge was*! He had first appeared in Salt Lake City on this bridge. The time-door must be on this bridge!

He put the Porsche in gear, swung it around, and roared back the way he had just come. And nothing happened. He merely came to the end of the bridge. He hit the brakes, swerved, repeated the process, going to the other end of the highway bridge and back several times. He even tried it on the wrong side of the road, against traffic, chickening out a few more hapless drivers.

Still nothing. Sirens were wailing everywhere now. He swerved to the right side of the roadway, and took an exit. He tore down several side streets until he found a warehouse district and stopped the car. The pounding in his ears was his heartbeat. They would be looking for his car now. He'd walk back to the dump, get the compound gun back that he gave Barrelman.

As he walked back, using the under-the-elevated-highway route, he tried to figure out why he couldn't go back to his own time.

Wait a minute! If the time-storm that had brought him to Salt Lake City had been *created* by the nuke war—no wonder he couldn't get back! The nuke war hadn't happened yet! There *was* no time-tunnel! What he had tried to do was impossible. For now.

Rockson reasoned, logically, that he'd have to wait until the exact date and time of the nuke attack—September 11, 1989, 6:04 P.M. Central Standard Time—and then try again to break through the damned Veil. He'd do his best to take Kim and his kids and his friends with him too. He'd try to save them from destruction.

When Rockson reached the dump, Barrelman handed him back his weapon.

"Told you so," he said. "But you sure tried—I'll hand you that. Never saw a car go so fast!"

"Maybe you know *now* how determined a guy I am," Rock said. "Help me destroy the Chessman."

"I can't do that!" Barrelman looked down. "Sorry."

"Then, I'll fight alone," Rock snarled. "You make me sick. You eat their garbage, live like hunted rats, yet you will not fight."

Rock turned to leave but Barrelman shoved a piece of worn colored paper at him—a map. Rockson looked at the old, worn-out Exxon road map. The heavily creased map was a treasure. It looked like the Salt Lake City map Rock remembered from the Century City archives.

The map showed Interstate 15 and Interstate 80, coursing north-south and east-west respectively, the highways cut through the heart of the fabled city of Joseph Smith, the great religious figure of the early western expansion of the United States.

To think that this holy city now housed such an abomination as the Chessman, thought Rockson.

The garbage dump he stood in now was in the south, the rundown Park Terrace section of the city. He should be able to see Mt. Olympus, elevation 9026 feet. It was a clear day. Yet all he saw looking southeast was haze. Back to the problem at hand: Rockson had to get across town again. According to Barrelman's running commentary as the Doomsday Warrior surveyed the crumbling, taped-together Exxon map, it would be easier if he went up along the elevated highway.

"The cameras are fewest there. Then you'll see the signs for Route One-eighty-one. Then you'll pass the planetarium—look for the dome. Watch out around there. It's a favorite haunt of the rookies. Why not stay with us?"

"And eat garbage? I'm going. I'll die a Freeman, or I will triumph—for myself and all of you."

"Well, then, if I can't stop you, friend . . ." Barrelman pulled out a set of keys—all corroded. "Here.

Take these keys. At Eleventh Avenue and Charles Street there's a corner shop — it used to be mine. The sign, if it's still there, reads HOBBIE SHOP. Model planes in the window, if those are still there — I think they are. The consultants only recently came out against hobbies. They now say people should not waste their time, that people should work more instead. Anyway, no one dared open it after they came in the middle of the night and threw me out of it. Inside the store are some things you might want. A knife — a big hunting knife. It used to be my dad's. It's in a box stuck up under the rear part of the counter, if they haven't found it. There's a sink if you need water — and you will, today's hot."

There was a perfectly geometric grid of pink and gray squares all across the map of the city, sixty-four in all. Rockson asked Barrelman what they were.

"Those are the control squares. After the coup, the one that made Chessman mayor, he had a block of buildings torn down every ten blocks, and had a large flower bed and walk area of cobblestones put in its place. Lots of the homeless are a result of that housing demolition. Each square has the same name as a chessboard square — you know, like King's Three, or Queen's Seventh. It's another way that Chessman controls the city. It's hard to go too far without crossing one of the squares. And the poles all around the squares have sensing devices — cameras with zoom lenses, microphones, the works. We avoid the squares if possible, wind our way around the city. But it slows you down if you're in a hurry."

Rock sighed. The evil control of this Chessman knew no bounds. Nearly total social control — that was what he had accomplished. Like on the TV programs Rock had watched with Kim. *Twenty questions* . . . only one answer: social order.

Barrelman confirmed that the Chessman lived in the Tabernacle most of the year, though sometimes in the winter he "castled," meaning he moved to City Hall Tower, across town. Barrelman said, "If you manage to kill the Chessman, destroy the radio tower above the bell tower in the Tabernacle, too. That's where the muzic comes from. Remember, use the key to my store, hole up there until late night. Don't try to get into the Tabernacle in the daylight. Best time to try to get into the Tabernacle is probably midnight mass. Incidentally, you don't have a chance."

"Midnight mass? Does the Tabernacle still have religious services?" Rockson asked, ignoring the negative remark.

Barrelman smiled. "Not the usual kinds. They are all banned. *Compassion* is banned—you should know that. To feel for another citizen except in certain ways, like in marriage, is illegal. People don't realize—can't realize—that soon they will be homeless too. There are practically no jobs, except construction. The city must grow—upward. Housing for the rich, death for the poor. Have you seen how they clear a building they want to tear down?"

"It's very vivid in my memory."

"Yes . . . Good! So wait in my store, and join the flock that goes through the Temple Square—now called King's Two Square—at midnight." Barrelman motioned with his arm. "Come over to the crate I call home; I have something for you." Rockson followed. The derelict reached in a corner of a packing crate

116

and extracted a red suit. "You'll need this—it's a bit the worse for wear, but it will be dark . . . If you need to hide, there's six or seven empty marble crypts in the left aisle of the Tabernacle. The covers are heavy, but they can be moved by a man with strength.

"You know, years ago, I went with my family—they're all dead now—to the Tabernacle. That was back when things were different. There was a heavenly choir there. Beautiful voices raised in praise to the Almighty. The singing is strange now, with weird, disjointed music. A devil's mass, I suppose. But you'll see. Good luck. And listen . . . if you can, be sure to put out the radio tower. Possibly I can get the other homeless people to rise up if you can put out the damned muzic."

Barrelman hugged the Doomsday Warrior. "I think you're the bravest American I ever met, and I'll see you Off the Board, in the Great Whatever."

"I'm not planning to die just yet, Barrelman!"

Rockson set off, having donned the old suit. It wasn't a bad fit—a big man had worn it. But the previous owner had obviously been endowed with a pot belly, for Rockson had to cinch the rope belt tight to keep his pants on.

He walked over the mounds of garbage and toward the elevated highway that bordered the edge of the dump, as Barrelman had directed. Lost in the inky shadows of the big roadway, he passed a few broken surveillance cameras mounted on concrete pillars under the road. Evidently falling debris—bolts and nuts from the speeding vehicles—had put out their eyes.

Perhaps the city fathers didn't think it very important to replace the cameras, as they'd only be broken again. Moving quickly under the highway till it began getting lower to ground level, Rockson crossed half the distance back through town unobserved. Barrelman, even if he wouldn't help directly, had given him a map, a key, a *chance*.

Chapter 10

Eddie spotted his quarry even before it appeared as a blip on the glowing radar screen on his instrument panel.

By squinting and straining his small, close-set eyes, he could just barely make out its pale shape as it hovered near the foot of an elm tree. Or, rather, what had once been a magnificent green elm back in the old days, back before the Dutch Elm blight had turned Salt Lake City's parks into a pathetic forest of stumps and fallen branches.

No time for these maudlin thoughts. Eddie jerked himself to attention, swung his tanklike vehicle around, and began lowering its long vacuum arm in line with the target.

"Stay right there, you sucker. You're gone. I'm gonna blow you away," Eddie muttered under his breath. Sweat poured down his face as he took aim. With a quiet beep, the radar let him know that he was on target: the enemy fluttered helplessly in the center of his sights. The autofocus headlamps illuminated it.

He threw his vehicle into gear, let up on the clutch,

and stomped on the gas pedal to lurch quickly into firing range.

"Aaaaaiieee." He bellowed a karate yell as he slammed his hand down on the attack button. The vacuum arm hissed, sucking in its victim and swallowing it to some dark place in the vehicle's gut.

Eddie punched the destroy button, then relaxed his tense muscles, wiped the sweat from his forehead, and sat back smugly to listen to the sound of the brush-eater's mighty tearing teeth as they shredded his quarry—a pizza box obviously left under the tree by a group of litterbugs who didn't appreciate social order.

Shiftless scum. These lowlife wasted their time hanging around the park, leaving their trash behind them like the wake of a garbage scow. Don't know the meaning of work. Or dignity.

Eddie knew what dignity was. It was a thing you didn't have, back in the old days, if you were a small man, barely five foot four, and you worked for the Salt Lake City Parks Department wearing a baggy olive-drab jumpsuit, slogging through the parks day after day, dragging a garbage bag behind you and spearing trash on a long, pointed stick.

Then had come the coup that changed Salt Lake City for the better. The glorious, wonderful Chessman, had been rebuilding a new world of glass towers on the ruins of the old. It was the Chessman who had given Eddie his dignity, given him twenty-five tons of high-tech machinery to replace his garbage bag and stick, and given him a smart, epauletted uniform to replace the sagging jumpsuit. As his first act under the new regime, Eddie had revved up his brush-eater, trained its sites on his old jumpsuit, which lay like a heap of rags on the ground, and then he'd ground it up to a total oblivion. Since that time, Eddie—now Sergeant Eddie of the Salt Lake City Parks Police Force—spent six nights out of seven on patrol, vigilantly searching out the litter that threatened to destroy his parks.

After his battle with the pizza box, which now lay shredded in the belly of the mechanical beast that all criminals feared, he switched on the radio. There was no choice of country-western, light rock, jazz or classical music these days. Each station now broadcast only the proper music of the Chessman regime, or, as in this case, announcers exhorting pawns to work hard, to spend their money on houses, cars, furs, and the other goods that would help bring the economy back to life. And it warned them always to shun the unclean.

"Cleanliness is next to godliness," Eddie recited his mother's credo. He could remember her only with a bar of soap and a pail of water as she scrubbed endlessly the dishes, the floors, the clothes, and Eddie himself. He embraced the cleanliness part of it, but rejected the godliness. Belief in God had gotten his mother nowhere, especially after the economy faltered. She'd slowly rotted away from the toil and was finally done in by a teen mugger.

"Cleanliness is next to Chessmanness," Eddie substituted. He would always be faithful to his mother and to Chessman. Eddie would scour the park night after night, searching and destroying the detritus that threatened the very heart of the Salt Lake City civilization, circa 1989.

121

"Dirty people have dirty minds; they contaminate our society with their filth," the voice on the radio droned on and on through Eddie's shift. With its soft *zzzzzttttt, zzzzzttttt,* the brusheater wheeled through the park, sucking up beer cans, soda bottles, old newspapers, paper bags, and half-eaten sandwiches. When the first traces of dawn struggled out, Eddie swung back toward the Park Police garage, where his machine disgorged its digested load. Then he went to bed in his small room, staring at the ceiling tiles, which were red and white in chessboard pattern, until he fell asleep.

The sounds of birds twittering in the leaves woke Rosa from her sleep. At least, in her drowsiness, it *sounded* like the song of birds. Actually, it was just a dead tree limb scratching against another limb in the hot wind that was stirred to life as the sun appeared.

She sat up, then gathered the rags that served as a bed, stuffing them into an old Zion Co-op shopping bag that looked like it couldn't last out another rainstorm. Oh, well, thought Rosa, who was inclined to look on the bright side, since it's a heat wave, it seems unlikely that we'll have rain any time soon.

As an optimist, she spent much of her time counting the blessings that life had bestowed upon her. She was still young, only twenty-five, and had kept a nice figure. Curves where they should be, tight muscles where they belonged. She knew she was attractive, and she liked to laugh a lot. Her health, well, maybe it had gone down a little after the bulldozers took down her apartment building, leaving her homeless, but she was still strong. She had a soft spot to put her bed every night. And best of all, she had a colony of good friends to live with, among them that most special person, Karl, who had recently become her lover.

If Rosa were the kind of person to count the bad things about her life, she might have noted that she was homeless, living in a little shantytown of cardboard boxes, packing crates, and tarps surrounded by piled brush in Pioneer Park. She might also have recalled that the Chessman and his cronies called her ilk "shifless vagrants" and "untouchables," and that his rookies sometimes rounded them up from the doorways and sidewalks, and beat them or threw them in the dump. She might also have remembered that there were lots of homeless people — friends of hers, as well as strangers — who seemed to just disappear into the night. Where did they go? Into the desert? Swallowed up by the great Salt Lake? It was best not to think about that.

"Rise and shine. It's going to be a beautiful sunny day," Rosa said, shaking Karl, whose snores rose from his newspaper bed next to hers. When his snores turned to snorts, Rosa got up and went to the little lean-to the group jokingly called the kitchen, to get a morning cup of coffee. It was a rare treat Rosa had scavenged from the new glass office towers: partly drunk cups of coffee left by office workers; cold coffee brought back to the shantytown to reheat for breakfast.

She brought a cup back to Karl, who was invisible except for a single arm groping out from under a sheet of newspaper. His hand looked like a crawling spider as it felt around for an empty bottle of port wine lying nearby, and the sight made Rosa giggle.

"Have this instead, honey," she said as she substituted the steamy coffee for the wine bottle. "You'll need your energy today. Remember? It's Carmella's birthday. We gotta get some money so we can have a party and buy her a nice yam cake."

Karl grunted, then sat up, shaking pages of the *Salt Lake Daily Reporter* from him. He grabbed Rosa, pulled her to him, and gave her a passionate kiss. Rosa stopped laughing long enough to kiss him back.

"Rosita, my little Rosita, how about a little—"

"Not now, babe." She pushed his hand from her breast. "Maybe later, after we get Carmella's cake."

"Can I lick the icing?" Karl teased as he licked her nose and eyelids. They both knew getting a cake wouldn't be easy.

"Karl wants to have his cake and eat it too," joked an overweight, white-bearded man who had just emerged from a nearby packing crate. Despite his soiled and tattered clothes, the dignified way he held himself reminded the other shantytown inhabitants of a college teacher. "The Professor," they'd dubbed him, and his packing-crate home was nicknamed "the campus."

By this time, the other residents were beginning to stretch and rise from their various cartons, crates, ragpiles, and newspapers. A number of scrawny dogs and bony cats began to sniff around for a bite of food or a friendly pat. The whole shantytown, hidden in the dense copse of dead elms, was awakening.

"Rosita! Rosita! Look what I found last night—a birthday present for Carmella." Angie shouted from

124

her last own "home" thirty feet away. She was holding in front of her the mangy yet somehow appealing remnant of a fur coat, now about as patchy as the fur of the yard dogs.

"I found it in the trash of one of the new apartment buildings. A rookie came up just as I was pulling it out of the garbage can, and I thought for sure he had me. I couldn't decide whether to drop the coat and run, or keep it and maybe be caught," she laughed. "So I kept hold of it, and started complaining that the missus always throws things out, then sends me down and makes me go through the trash to get them back. I complained so loud he believed me, thought I was the maid, and didn't try to arrest me."

Amused, her audience applauded Angie's quick thinking and courage. She tossed the coat over her shoulders and began prancing up and down the yard, turning like a fashion model on a runway. "Hey Professor, how does this look?"

"Angie's hot stuff now. You need a limousine to take you to your restaurants and parties," the Professor said. He wheeled a rusted wire shopping cart to the center of the short alley between the homes. "Please step aboard, madam." He bowed and took her hand. "Your car is ready."

Angie clambered into the cart, the fur coat still dangling from her shoulders, and the Professor spun her around the yard to the laughter and shouts of the colony.

They pulled to a halt in front of Rosa, and the Professor gallantly helped Angie from the shopping cart. Rosa hugged her enthusiastically, and ran her fingers through the patches of fur remaining on the coat. "It's beautiful. And it's just what Carmella needs to keep her warm on winter nights. Angie, you did great. We're going to send you to do all our shopping."

Rosa, the Professor, and Angie set out after a short while to earn the money needed to buy Carmella a birthday pie. There were few stores that would sell anything to a homeless person, even if they had money. But Carmella deserved the best, and that, said Angie, was what she was gonna get.

They would buy Carmella one of Auntie Marsha's delicious—and large—yam cakes. The steaming hot cakes were sold out of an abandoned bakery in Ryder Alley, near Pioneer Park. Of course, Marsha didn't have a permit to operate a bakery, but the apparently-boarded-up store did a thriving trade late in the evening. The old heavyset black Marsha, with her huge white apron and white kerchief tying up her pigtails, made the best cake. The cakes didn't have any of those Chessman hypo-drugs in them either. Marsha was unlicensed, so she didn't have to do that.

The cake was only two dollars, but that was a lot of money. And there was only one way to get it—collect all the discarded soda and beer cans around the construction sites downtown and bring them to the Acme Supermarket parking lot. In the parking lot was a machine that digested the cans and spat a five-cent piece out for each one. The trouble was, digging in the garbage for discarded cans was illegal, by the Chessman's edict. To be caught could mean a stint on *Twenty Questions*, the notorious TV torture-quiz

126

program.

But Angie was quick, and the Professor and Rosita were good lookouts. They had collected the cans many times before without incident. And the small group of homeless had thrived, sharing in the relative wealth that the can collection created.

That night, at about eleven P.M., the little encampment of packing crates and lean-tos in the middle of the park was the scene of a jolly, if restrained, party. A single candle was lit on the hot yam cake that had been cut carefully into twelve sections, one for every member of the community. Carmella, dressed in her best dress—a "previously owned" but repaired house frock with a floral red design—blew out the candle. She was forty-one and toothless, but her smile was like that of a young happy child. She had *friends*. What if she had no "real" place to live? The encampment in the park was pleasant enough. And if they were very careful with the lights, only using the battery flash when absolutely necessary, the thick brush and fallen tree limbs they had encircled their makeshift community with would protect them against discovery.

It was indeed better than the city dump, where more and more of the city's homeless were being crowded. In some ways, the little park community was better than the condos too. At least the company was better. Warm, charming people, not cold rich snobs. Real people, who would give you the shirt off their backs.

It was with those thoughts running through her

127

mind that Carmella thanked them all for their presents and especially for the cake. They all took their pieces and began to eat. It was delicious, and the passed-around bottle of port wine was just the thing to rinse it down with.

Eddie was out again this night, his big machine roaring up to full speed in its sixth gear. The mad-eyed driver of the brush-eater stared at the park ahead through his windshield, occasionally looking at the sweep of the green line around the litter-detector radar screen in the dashboard. *There.* There directly ahead — a pie box. Another pizza box? No, as his headlights brought the object clearly into his sights, Eddie saw that this was one of those taller white cake boxes. A birthday-cake box.

What was it doing so far into this park? People didn't even like to walk here, so far from the street-lights. It was creepy here, and full of debris — thick debris.

He twisted the gearshift, wrenching the machine to low. The twisting cutters and suction arm of the Parks vehicle engaged the box and tore it up and digested it — along with a good part of the turf under it. *There.* That's better, he thought.

He was about to back off, for the vehicle was nearly dead up against the thicket of brush and fallen elm branches. But he hesitated. There hadn't been any other litter in the park; he probably wouldn't come across any for the rest of the night. He'd been too efficient these past few nights, too good. Perhaps it was time to tackle the harder job — clearing the damned tangles of brush and branches that loomed before him. *Yeah*, that's a job that would last the night!

The Professor was the first one to notice. The city had a din to it — traffic, the all-night music pouring from its lightpole speakers — but *this* sound was different. Throatier. *Closer.*

Everyone held their breath, sat motionless on the spread-out picnic blanket, staring into the dark.

"There," whispered the professor, "over there!"

The group's twenty-four eyes turned as one, spotted the searchbeam of the huge machine Eddie was hurtling at the nestlike thicket to the north.

"*Brusheater*," Rosita screamed, dropping her last piece of yam cake and hurtling up and away from the danger. The others, too, arose in panic. But there was only one way in or out of the head-high, carefully piled, impenetrable tangle of twigs and sticks. One little alley led to the little village — and the brusheater was chewing its way down that narrow alley right now, its blinding searchbeam sweeping from side to side, its huge metal teeth and rotating scissor-jaws chomping away at the wood.

"We're dead meat," whimpered Karl.

"No!" yelled the Professor. "Don't panic. I'll tell you what to do!" He gave rapid instructions: "Take the packing crates apart, start throwing them one after the other on top of the thick brush, make some sort of bridge over the tangle away from the brush-eater. That way we can scramble over the debris to safety!"

It worked, though it was wobbly. Most of them made it. But not the Professor. He was old, and he was also brave, determined that the others would live, even if he should die. He picked up a thick branch, wider than the yawning jaws of the brusheater, and walked toward it. "Stop," he yelled, jamming the thick branch into its yard-wide grin. "Stop. You are destroy—"

He never finished. The gears ground, the jaws snapped the thick branch as if it were a toothpick, and the suction, like a hurricane, drew the Professor into the gullet of *hell*.

Laughing madly, Eddie continued his work. What a find! A whole fucking village of the derelict bastards. That'd teach 'em. The bastards thought they'd use the park as a fuckin' condo, did they? Didn't want to pay no rent, did they?

I'll get a medal for this, he thought. A damned fucking big medal . . .

Rosita, sobbing, held onto Karl's shoulder as the big man, holding the flashlight, led the others east, then south, down the midnight-drizzly streets of the city. "Ain't no place for us now," she sobbed. "The Professor is dead, and there ain't no place for us now except the city dump."

They all knew she was right.

Chapter 11

Rock looked up at the sign. He was on King's Street, close to King's Three Square. He'd been zigzagging through the city, using the twisting streets, avoiding the squares, as Barrelman had suggested. The going had been slow: the streets were filled with housewives picking up groceries and goods from the official city-run stores—the only stores still operating in the city. Rockson stood out like a beacon, being practically the only man in the streets at the shopping hours. He decided he might as well chance the direct approach through the last two squares planted with roses—the King's Squares. People came there just to look at the beautiful red flowers—women *and* men.

The Chessman had these squares especially wired for camera surveillance. Every time you set foot in a square you were on camera. Only by moving through the side streets around the square could you avoid being tracked by computer. But he was in disguise, after all. And impatient. Rockson, despite Barrelman's warnings, plunged into the King's Three Square.

High above him, on the light stancions, tiny cameras began to turn, locking onto the man moving at too fast a clip.

King's Three Square was, indeed, more evenly sprinkled with both sexes. Looking at the flowers was practically a patriotic duty. The red roses were well-tended, aromatic. He soon realized he was walking a lot faster than anyone else. He slowed down. The camera watching him was not fooled, however. It kept him in its sight. Rockson, trying to blend in, paused at a bridal shop along with a group of citizens. The animated window dummies, a lifelike man and woman wearing Victorian dress, were depicted having a nice evening at home. The man-dummy was smoking his pipe; the dog, complete with mechanical wagging tail, was eating his Ruffy dog food. The woman was baking bread, opening and shutting the old oven. The speaker in the window said, "*Domestic life can be blissful! Listen to the Chessman, find a suitable mate, and get married today*! Otherwise, *you might end up as a street person and get eaten by the brush-eaters.*" A rookie car cruised past. As soon as the rookie car turned the corner, Rockson took off again toward the Tabernacle.

He had just entered King's Two Square when he noticed everyone had suddenly stopped walking. They were standing there looking up at the speakers mounted over the elaborate rosebeds. Rock, who had used all his mental powers to ignore the hypnotic music, now let himself hear. Something was up.

"*We interrupt this program of exciting elevator muzik to warn all citizens that the psycho-stalker is at large again. All Squad Nine red knights go to King's Two Square to apprehend suspect.* Warning! *He could be armed. Shoot to kill. Repeat, shoot to kill!"*

Rockson realized he'd be spotted. People looked around fearfully; he saw the startled looks of those that set eyes on him as his description was broadcast.

"The psycho could be dressed as you are, but he has distinctive features — a white streak through his black hair; and mismatched blue eyes, one light, one dark. His build is very good, he is very tanned and is tall, over six feet two inches. Do not attempt to apprehend. When the red knights appear, point at the psycho."

Rock turned and began running back the way he came, but from around a corner came a galloping squad of red knights. "*Halt in the name of the law,*" one shouted. Their weed-burners came up, leveled at Rockson. He wasn't going to halt, and he wasn't going to be a target of those mini-flamethrowers either!

He threw the jacket aside, uncovering his compound gun. He began blasting it across the squad of horsemen, barreling at him like the Apocalypse itself. The faceshields shattered, the riders fell from their saddles. The horses ran riderless and smashed into the "Victorian family" window. And then their weed-burner tanks, which had been hit by Rock's bullets and had started leaking, ignited. Some fool knight had tried to fire his leaky flame-weapon. The spark set off an explosion. Flaming knights came screaming every which way. Rock cut them down mercifully with a short burst of bullets, then he ran past the conflagration and around a corner—only to be confronted by shouting voices and pointing fingers: "There he is, in the shirt with no jacket! He's got a gun!" People pointed out a window—a young couple and a kid screamed, "There he is, get him, get the homeless bastard."

Rock didn't waste any ammo on them, for he saw who they were shouting to—a block further down the narrow street, heading toward him on motorcycles, were a half dozen rookies. And between him and these agents of death was a woman pushing a baby carriage. She had just left the curb, and was frozen in fear.

"Get the hell out of the line of fire, lady," Rock yelled, but before she could, the rookies on the cycles opened up with their bike-mounted cannons. The shells riddled the lady and the baby carriage. Pieces of flesh and blood and bone blew up into the air. A series of holes opened up in the wall behind and above Rockson. He rolled and dove and rolled again until he was sheltered by a parked Buick. The big blue car's back door took a hit, absorbed it. Rock jumped up and let loose a volley, now that he had no more worries about innocent bystanders.

The riders were jerked like rag dolls off their seats in a spatter of seared flesh. The bikes spun away, one skidding right by Rock's booted foot. "He killed the cops," a hysterical voice yelled from above. "Get him, get the homeless bastard."

In seconds, the streets were lousy with red knights and rookies as distress signals went out all over the city.

"Clear the streets . . . Citizens, clear the streets

. . . *Your lives are in danger,*" the public-address system ordered as panic gripped the King's Two Square area. Throngs of people scurried for cover while a horde of police closed in on the sector.

Rock unloaded round after round into the waves of advancing knights. The pile of horseflesh and moaning humans grew in front of him. Finally, the barrel of his compound gun grew so hot that it glowed red, and it seized up on him. As the attackers clambered over the pile of dead and dying on each end of the street, Rockson pulled open the front door of the big Buick. No key. With the butt end of his gun, he smashed the ignition apart, reached in and pulled out the wires, stripped them with his knife, and made the right connections.

The Buick was in motion, though half its rear was gone. It was a dinosaur of a car, a relic from the heydays of the 1980s when gas was cheap and the living was easy. Familiarizing himself with the gears, Rock lurched the car forward, the wheels of the powerful, heavy vehicle chewing up the pavement. Another dozen riders with weed-burners galloped toward him. Rock hit the floorboard with the accelerator: he'd have to go right past his "friends." The wheels spun and screeched. A bath of flames drenched the old battle wagon but it was too late to stop her. Rock had broken out again, leaving practically every cop in town behind in a mass of confusion, pain, and death.

Rockson felt the big Buick accelerate smoothly through the empty streets, taking corners at 60 mph, careening through newstands, erasing fire hydrants, and hurling rows of garbage cans at buildings. Red knights and rooks passed by heading in the opposite direction, the car—which had lost its muffler—zipping past before they could react.

Rockson threw his head back and roared in a wild laugh, catching sight of his frenzied countenance in the rear-view mirror. He screeched the car to a stop and hunched over the steering wheel in exhaustion, breathing deeply. Then he looked at himself in the mirror again.

"What in God's name is this place! I sure as hell hope it's a dream, because I would like to wake up . . ."

He knew he couldn't stay in the car. They had certainly been tracking him through the city's sophisticated monitor system, and he wouldn't get far without a fight. He had to lay low and think up a better plan.

He'd fired too eagerly—he needed ammo. And a little to drink wouldn't hurt either. He turned a corner, screeched to a halt.

"Thanks for the ride, old buddy," he said to the Buick as he kicked the door shut. "I'll say one thing—they sure don't make 'em like you anymore. I'll bet I could take out the whole Russian army with fifty battle wagons like you."

Casting a catlike glance over his shoulder, Rock grabbed his submachine gun and sprang into an alleyway, disappearing from the Chessman's monitors.

While the red knights and the rooks disentangled themselves from the debacle at King's Two Square, Rockson scavenged through the basements of a row of closed shops, preparing himself for the battles to come. From a bookstore, he took a pocket guide to the city, taking a few moments to orient himself and plan possible avenues of escape.

The basements were connected by a series of heavy iron doors secured with padlocks. Rock thought it strange that the entire neighborhood was deserted as he passed from cellar to cellar, blasting the locks apart with single shots from his weapon. He moved from the bookstore to a delicatessen, grabbing a nice salami—preserved food—drank a beer, then hit a hardware store where he picked up a set of bolt-cutters.

Unfortunately he found no gun shop to replenish his dwindling supply of submachine-gun ammo. He took stock and found he had about four hundred rounds left. A sporting goods store did provide him with some extra firepower, however. There were no sophisticated weapons, but he grabbed a shotgun, stuffing a handful of cartridges into his pocket, and selected a handsome bowie knife which he sheathed in his belt.

Back at Kings Two Square, the Chief of Rooks and the Master of the Horse arrived to take charge of the failing pursuit. The men were ordered to fall in on the grounds of the public square where their officers calmed them and formed them into squads.

"Men, we have this fugitive isolated and we're not going to let him slip out of our grip again," announced the Master of the Horse, field commander of the red knights. "He's killed enough of us and single-handedly paralyzed the entire city. It's a question of pride now. We're gonna have to dig a lot of graves for our fellow officers he's killed. Do you intend to let him get away with it?" The master's blubbery face shook in anger.

The entire square erupted in a tumultuous roar. "No" they screamed, some three hundred men raising their voices at once. A huge truck pulled up. Men started unloading weaponry.

"All right," interjected the Chief of Rooks, field general of that corps. "Now listen up. Here's how we'll handle it . . ." Soon each rookie was given a submachine gun and some clips. Then a large chart with a layout of the city was unfolded and taped high on a wall. The chief approached with a pointer and began laying out the plan of attack.

"We've traced him to this point," he said, indicating the spot where Rockson had abandoned the Buick. "Now he's on foot and he hasn't shown up on any monitors since. So he can't be far. Here's the plan. The rooks will put a perimeter force here, along here, here, and here . . ." he said, encircling a thirty-block area with the pointer. "It will be our job to make sure the maniac doesn't escape. It's an old area. We're prepared to sacrifice this entire section of the city if need be, but under no circumstances can we let that man escape from this sector. The rooks will form into three columns and follow these avenues to their positions. All right, all rooks see your sergeants immediately to find out exactly where your station is. Move out *Now!*"

With that, the rooks were quickly dispatched to their stations, in an attempt to encircle the enemy. The hundred knights were given RPG-7 grenade launchers.

When the rooks had departed and the chief taken his position at communications headquarters to monitor his troops and watch for signs of Rockson, the Master of the Horsemen began detailing his order of battle for the red knights.

"All right, men, he's our baby. I want him alive if at all possible, but that's *not* necessary. We'll divide up into squads of sixteen and conduct a house-to-house search of the entire sector. As you approach each house, use your discretion as to how to handle the search. I suggest leaving half the squad to guard the entrances while the other half enters the building and searches, but use your own judgment for each individual building. Remember, this bastard is *dangerous*! If you suspect the fugitive is in a particular building, don't hesitate to use the RPGs to flush him out. Use the weed-burners on the wooden structures. We're in no big hurry. The rooks have the streets blocked, so this guy ain't going anywhere. Sooner or later, he'll turn up. When conducting your search, keep in voice contact with each other—and, sergeants, keep in contact with the base. All channels have been cleared for this operation. Any questions?"

"Sir?" replied one sergeant in the square, "what about civilians? Has the area been cleared so they won't get in our way?"

"As much as possible under the circumstances. I'm sure there are stragglers, and evacuation is not total. In any case the prime objective is the capture of the psycho. Don't let *anything* stand in the way of that. Is that clear? Social order must be maintained."

"Yes sir," replied the sergeant with a snappy salute.

"One more thing, men—I said I want this guy alive if possible. As you know, we need more contestants for the *Twenty Questions* quiz program. If he doesn't give himself up freely upon sight, your orders are to shoot to kill, though. I don't want him pulling any tricks. One more thing—we might have to smoke this guy out, and there's not going to be good visibility in that case. Don't shoot each other. Chessman loves you! Remember your training, and *let's get him*! A promotion of three full grades awaits every member of the team that captures him, dead or alive. Now let's *Go*!"

A roar erupted from the corps of knights, incensed by the thought of the psycho who had wasted their fellow officers. They held their weapons over their heads and shouted again before mounting their horses and cantering into the battle zone to begin their search.

"We'll find him, sure," one knight bantered to a nearby rider, "then we'll all be promoted."

"In a pig's eye," the other red knight responded. "I myself will get that homeless bastard. I've got ten that says I do!"

"You're on!"

The search began within minutes. The ranks of red knights passed through the outer files of rooks, the men eager to swing into action after weeks of routine patrolling.

It quickly became an ugly affair. Trigger-happy

140

from the start, the squads took their orders to be a passport for looting and wanton destruction. They adopted the technique of simply torching buildings before even searching — looking to burn the fugitive out into the open rather than risk their lives in a close search. Citizens caught in the zone were shown little quarter, the rooks on the perimeter taking potshots at anything not wearing the distinctive uniform of the red knights. Anyone caught unaware within the sector was simply wasted before they could even identify themself. A cloud of smoke began to rise over the troubled quarter as fires spread for house to house and from store to store.

It didn't take Rockson long to realize the heat was on. He carefully loaded and watched as the cordon of rooks deployed and the red knights began their search. Hiding inside the sporting-goods store, he could see the vast numbers of horsemen galloping up and down the street as columns of smoke rose everywhere. He ran to the back of the store and peered through a small window in a bathroom. Two doors down, a team of horsemen waited while their companions kicked in a door and went in, their RPGs flaming before them. Rockson ran to the stairwell leading back to the basement, but smoke was already collecting there from fires in neighboring buildings. He could hear the screams of citizens caught in the path of the destruction.

Rockson had no sooner turned back up the stairs when the front door of the store was kicked in and a blast of flames erupted in his face, singeing his skin.

His arm jerked up instinctively and released a salvo from the 16-gauge automatic shotgun he had collected. He hit one rookie with a broadside to the head, splattering the man's cerebral matter into the face of his partner, who entered laughing right behind him. He had no sooner wiped it off when Rockson charged the door and caught the man's neck with a flying scissors kick that snapped his spinal column instantly. Rock tumbled to his feet and out the door, discharging the shotgun in a circle of blasts, sending three more rooks to hell. A red knight galloped up. Rock tore him from his mount, then pulled himself up on a wild-eyed white stallion as it galloped past and sunk his heels deep into the horse's ribs, sending it charging through the streets. Squads of horsemen began closing in on him from all directions. The entire section of the city was erupting in senseless violence. Citizens caught in the melee were running for their lives, leaping from windows of burning buildings and diving to escape being trampled by the rampaging horsemen. The red knights were now out of control. Caught in the frenzy of the moment, they were blasting their RPG-7s at anything that moved. The public speakers blared with confusing and contradictory orders. Knights galloping one way ran into rooks moving the opposite way, and in the confusion, arguments and disorder swept through the ranks.

Rockson was riding the gauntlet like a pro, his steed not spooked by the raging fires and the screams of burning people. He emptied his shotgun at a band of knights caught off guard in an alley, then threw it aside, whipping his compound gun from his shoulder, employing it with murderous accuracy. But no sooner would he strafe down one squad of horsemen when another would appear galloping around a corner, inaccurately blasting away. Then, just as he thought himself breaking away, a solid line of rookie cars appeared, blocking the roadway, causing him to wheel about back into the fracas. He was riding with reckless abandon, shooting from the hip, his horse leaping fences and taking corners like a champion.

He turned onto a broad avenue with a score of knights in hot pursuit, their flaming weapons licking at his charger's long tail. Dead ahead, a roadblock stretched across the pavement. Old apartment buildings with bricked-up doorways lined the street — there was no escape. He would have to break the blockade.

He sped straight into the wall of vehicles, the galloping knights at his heels preventing the rooks from firing on him. Rockson stood high in the saddle and whispered into the ear of his foaming, frightened mount.

"One more jump, baby," he said calmly, "just give me one more *great big leap* and I'll take it from there."

He closed at breakneck speed. Everything depended on his horse. If he made the jump, he had a chance. If not, it was all over but the barbecue . . . literally.

Fifty yards to go, the barricade loomed larger and larger, the horse gasping for air, the knights gaining on him . . . forty yards and he could feel the heat at his back, his horse bursting its lungs in fear, a trickle of blood appearing at the beast's flaring nostrils . . .

thirty yards . . . twenty . . . ten . . . Rock screamed and stretched over the horse's neck, pulling it into its leap over the cars.

The rooks who had been lying flat on the roofs firing dove off as the horse stretched into a magnificent picture-book leap, reaching over the vehicles in a gracious arc. Rockson strained forward desperately. Would the horse make it, or—

The horse cleared the roadblock, but had given everything it had, and it came down on bent forelegs, throwing Rockson in a somersault over its head.

Rock had expected as much and rolled with his momentum, coming down a good fifteen yards past the barricade and rolling another ten yards before coming up firing, wiping out the band of rooks who stood with gaping mouths as the cruel weapon spit fire, cutting them to shreds. The mounts in pursuit were not up to the leap, those that tried crashing into the barricade, the others pulling up short as Rockson sprinted for cover.

Rock ran and ran, firing bursts at anything that moved. Finally, exhausted, bleeding, and thirsty, he ducked into a cellar well into another district. He'd hole up for a while. Like most stores in the city, this one was shut down. He went upstairs. It was a tailor shop—full of dusty clothing. He found several blue blazers and pants in the dim interior. On an inspiration, he looked for, and found, needle and thread. Later, dressed in consultant-like blazer and tan pants, he walked casually into the gathering night, the compound gun in a satchel made for tennis rackets. Again he headed toward the Tabernacle. He hoped that the black shoe dye he'd put in his hair worked as a disguise. The PA systems kept giving out his old description. He was ignored.

He tried to stay away from bright light — and from the blue-blazered thought police. It had taken him hours to sew on the insignia he had made with thread and a swatch of cloth. In the dark, the little medallion looked like the real insignia, although it wouldn't have passed close inspection. When he boldly strode into the Tabernacle Square — King's Square itself — and approached the church gate, he nodded and pointed to his medallion and the guards saluted. He joined the stream of midnight-mass attendees. He was walking up the steps with the others of high rank — the politicians, the higher cops, and some consultants — no women. This was a male-chauvinist society. He took a seat in one of the last pews inside the awesome cathedral. He had no plan except opportunity — he'd see what developed. Find a staircase. *Anything!* Besides, he wanted to hear this service — what would the midnight mass be? What was the midnight sermon that was supposed to be so special?

The red-robed bishops came in with candle-carrying altar boys. Like an old church service, Rockson thought. Not like the twenty-first-century religion of no sects. In the future it was all united — Buddhist, Christian, Hindu, Moslem: all meditated in the simple chapel at Century City.

There were at least a dozen priests, wearing black and clerical collars, on the wide altar. A half dozen or more preteen boys — acolytes — went around assisting them in the manipulation of religious articles.

The boys chanted up a storm of Latin, while the priests handed the articles and received them back from one tall red-robed man — the bishop, judging by his peaked hat. The priests and acolytes finished up their mystic business and left. The bishop climbed steps to a high, ornate pulpit with horrible wooden carvings — gargoyles. He put his figure into the light. He was narrow-faced, middle-aged, and wore thick horn-rimmed glasses. He cleared his throat and adjusted the microphone.

He began his sermon: "I am Bishop Pohsib. All ye gathered here know that it is not whether you win or lose, it's how you play the game. My talk tonight will dwell on that simple truth." He smiled, adjusted the microphone closer to his mouth, and continued. "My flock, know ye that it doesn't matter what square you occupy in the game of life, it is *how* you occupy that square . . ."

Applause.

"Ye are thanked . . . my flock, know ye that it doesn't matter if you are driven off the board, if the view is good on the way down . . .

Rockson only half listened after that point — it seemed to be drivel. Finally, after ten minutes of it, the topic became more interesting to him. After the bishop made the sign of the square and blessed all, he said: "It is with sadness that I report to you that His Holiness, Mayor Chessman, moved to City Hall Tower yesterday. He will spend the next few weeks working there while his suite upstairs is modernized."

A sigh of disappointment rolled through the gathered consultants and other solid citizens.

Shit, Rock thought, I've sneaked in here for nothing, risked all to penetrate the Tabernacle when Chessman *isn't even here*!

The lights came up. It was over. People got up and started to file out. Rockson decided to hide, and when all the audience had left, to still perform the second half of his mission. If he couldn't find and checkmate the Chessman tonight, he could *still* destroy the radio tower at the peak of the roof, and stop the mind-bending hypno-music.

He remembered Barrelman's advice that the marble crypts—heavy white coffins of stone carved with the same hideous gargoyles as the pulpit—demons with wings, hunchbacked twisted-faced dwarves with tridents—were advantageous places to hide. There were a half dozen along the left side of the vast room.

Rockson crouched and ran along the aisle until he could dash the ten feet to the nearest crypt, and with all his mutant strength pushed the heavy cover aside. Inside it was dark and cool and about four feet deep. Barrelman better be right, he thought as he jumped in, I sure hope to God these *are* empty. I don't want to get cozy with a bunch of bones right now.

Barrelman *wasn't* right. He landed in a crunchy pile of powdery bones, judging from the white dust. He was sure, when he struck a match for a brief instant to see. Only the skull seemed to be intact. The rest of the skeleton had completely disintegrated. Stifling a sneeze, he bent lower.

Oh, well, I've been in worse places, he thought.

Bending into a push-ups position over the corpse, he slid the cover back so that only a crack of light showed. Then he put his eyes to the opening. He could see the activity at the high altar. The bishop that had given the sermon, Bishop Pohsib, was dousing the thousands of candles with a long snuffer. A group of acolytes were helping him. If the six boys left, Rockson was determined to rush the high bishop, capture him, and wring some information from his lips. Information such as how to reach the radio tower, or maybe how to penetrate the City Hall Tower and get at Chessman. But for now, until the rigmarole upon the stage was completed, he would bide his time . . .

If this was like any of the ancient churches he'd read about, the bishop would perhaps have a go at a prayer alone before he left.

What the hell, it was a plan. And any plan was better than none. The compound gun was by his side; he'd soon make a move.

But the best-laid plans of churchmice and men sometimes go astray. Rockson heard what sounded like drums—no, not drums—footfalls in rhythm. A whole squad of synchro-stepping rookies, perhaps. Maybe they had *counted* the people who went into the church. Maybe they counted as everyone left, too and were *one* short!

Chapter 12

Rockson was desperate. Instead of catching the bishop, he himself was in risk of being caught, he realized. The crypt might become his tomb. The old marble coffin with carved gargoyles on the lid could become *his* coffin, if those tramping footsteps were what he suspected. But he'd take some with him!

Peering out from his crack, Rockson saw that the Tabernacle was crawling with armed rookies and thought police with trank-wands. Most of them wore helmets with mirrored visors that covered their faces. They were scurrying everywhere, as if they had caught his scent and were closing in for the kill. He had to get out. He reached in the darkness for the compound gun.

Suddenly the crack was filled with darkness, and Rock's vision was cut off. Someone was standing in front of the crack. Rockson drew back, diving for the darkness of the crypt—but it was too late. The lid was inching up, the view above filled with mirror-faced rookies.

Rockson reached for the compound gun, but before he could bring it up to fire, the long steel rod of a consultant slipped into the sarcophagus. Rockson felt its cold red tip touch his right sleeve. Instantly he was thrown into confusion. He was sprayed with a tranquilizer fluid from the long trank-wand.

He didn't know who he was, where he was. A rush of confused, disjointed thoughts rushed through his mind. And upon that wave of confusion was a powerful pleasant sensation, like sinking into mud while being sprayed with perfume—contradictory sensations. A smile broke out on his lips, and as the lid was fully removed, Rockson sat up.

"Hi, fellas," he said to the gathering of rookies and the consultant who now withdrew his weapon. "Wonderful, wonderful night, isn't it?"

The rookies were told to lower their weapons by the consultant. "He got a good dose," the consultant told them. "No need for guns now."

Rockson was asked to come out of the crypt. He did, dusting off the bone dust with his hands, still smiling. "It's fun in there—you should really try it sometime."

"Perhaps I will," said the consultant. "Now, you want to come with us, don't you?" No one looked into the dark reaches of the crypt. The compound gun was forgotten by Rockson also.

One of the rookies said, "Say, you don't suppose this is the freak that shot up half the town, do you?"

The consultant shook his head. "He doesn't fit the description—and he has no machine gun. He's just one of those church-break-in guys; some people adore Bishop Pohsib so much, they've got to see him in person."

Rockson was no longer smiling; instead his face

twitched. He realized he had been captured. "Some sort of drug in that—metal rod," he mumbled. "Where are you taking me?" The consultant sneered. In his icy, dead eyes, Rockson saw his own distorted reflection, moving up and down with the man's snapped-out words. "You have a great ability to withstand the drug. Pawns like you require treatment. You will get it."

"Treatment? What treatment?"

"You'll find out soon enough!" An officer grabbed Rockson's arms and pulled them behind his back, snapping on handcuffs. Then he shoved Rock toward the huge open door. "Move it!"

Rockson now understood that somehow he was thought of as a petty criminal. That was a break. Unless they found the gun, this might not be so bad. Kim would hear of his detention. And cute little Kim had bailed him out of trouble once before—perhaps she could do it again.

"My wife!" he exclaimed. "You must let me contact my wife. I have a right!"

"You have no rights under the law set forth by the Chessman."

"But you can vouch for me. I came to hear the bishop's talk—"

"She can't help you. Free thought is a serious offense. If the Chessman decides to release you, then you'll see her again. If He doesn't, you won't. You should have thought of that before you broke the law, mister. You're just lucky you're not carrying a weapon."

Rockson was about to protest further, but he was abruptly tranquilized. The consultant had again directed the trank-wand at him. It overpowered his own will and immobilized him. He felt as docile as a kitten.

He gave them a silly grin. "Whatever you say, fellas."

The watchful men led him out of the Tabernacle to their armored van waiting near Temple Square. They opened the rear door and threw him in. Three rookies followed him in and sat down on the benches on the sides of the van. They kept their weapons ready in case their prisoner, declared a "dangerous freethoughter" by their superior, should make the slightest move.

Rockson was not about to test their trigger fingers.

He shook his head and tried to sit up on the floor. A wave of hypno-music from inside the van covered him like a cool blanket, lulling him into a lethargic fog. It was the second-strongest music he'd heard since the time-tornado had dropped him in this bizarre place.

I must resist the music, he thought, but the free thought required too much effort. It was much easier to lie down and float into a color-filled, weightless void.

The soft, comforting hypno-music ended like a needle pulled from a record. Rockson was pulled from the van. Light-headed and feeling somewhat goofy, he blinked in the sunlight. To his left and in the distance, puffy little clouds drifted serenely over a heavy fog bank.

Before him rose an ominous, Gothic building made out of huge blocks of granite. CITY CONSULTANTS REHABILITATION CENTER was chiseled in the stone above the wide double doors. To the right of the doors was a brass plaque that read, *Dedicated to His Holy Highness, the Chessman.*

Rockson was taken through the doors. Inside, the building was dark with long, high-ceilinged halls that made every footstep and rustle echo loudly. The rookies ushered him to an elevator, which descended, Rockson thought, into the very bowels of the earth.

The elevator opened into a narrow hall marked by small, blank doors. The doors had no handles, but were opened by handprint. Ahead of him, Rockson saw a guard place his right hand on a sensor, then wait a few seconds while a computer scanned the print and matched it for authorization. The door opened and the guard stepped through. The door shut immediately behind him.

Rockson and his escorts walked on through the seemingly endless hall. Judging from the size of the facility, the Chessman was doing a lot of rehabilitating. His daze was wearing off — the muzik inside the building was much milder than in the van, and the trankwand's effect was wearing off.

At the end of the hall, the guards halted in front of a door built for midgets. An adult would have to stoop to go into and out of the room on the other side. One of the men activated the handprint lock. The door slid open and Rockson was shoved head first into an antiseptic cubicle.

The door shut behind him; he was alone. The room had no windows and a ceiling too high for him to reach. Even if he could have managed a jump — and he decidedly lacked the energy — there was nothing on the ceiling to grab onto, not even a light fixture. The ceiling itself seemed to glow, filling the cell with a harsh light that made Rockson squint. There was loud muzik—from a hidden speaker.

In one corner was a small toilet cemented into the floor. It was real, functioning plumbing, the kind Rockson had only seen in the quarters belonging to the privileged and rich in the condo areas. He realized he might be in this detention cell a long time. He checked everything—even the toilet. There was no lever or handle on it; Rockson guessed it flushed automatically. He tested his theory by pissing into it. The toilet flushed as soon as he was done.

There was no bed; he wondered why, and soon found out. As soon as he thought about bed and sleep, one wall started to ripple and open. A cot appeared and unfolded from the wall.

Rockson whistled. Slick. Was this illusion or what?

He felt the cot. It was real—or at least it *felt* real. He sat on it. It held his weight. He got up and dismissed thoughts of sleep. The cot dissolved into the wall.

He whistled again and ran his hands over the wall. There were no seams, no cracks. How in the hell did they do it?

There was only one explanation Rockson could accept—the hypno-music that filled his ears, seeming to come from everywhere. Reality was whatever you believed, and the lulling muzik was creating a new reality for him. It was programming him. He had to stop it!

He put his hands to his ears. He hummed. He talked out loud. Nothing blocked the insidious muzik.

"Hey!" he shouted. "Anybody out there? I know you're listening!"

There was no response but the flowing, mesmerizing hypno-music. Rockson knew his brain would have the equivalent of a lobotomy if he did not stop the muzik from penetrating his consciousness.

Then he remembered the Glowers — his teachers. Those strangely beautiful beings with their insides on the outside, organs pumping and throbbing away for the eye to see, their minds linked in telepathic thought. The Glowers generally kept to themselves, but had allowed Rockson to join their circle as a "learner," once, long ago — or rather a long time from now.

The Glowers had taught him many a survival technique for the mutated post-nuclear-war world. Perhaps, he thought, those same techniques would work in *this* world.

Rockson sat down on the cold cement floor and crossed his legs in a lotus position for meditation. It required supreme mental effort, as the hypno-music was steadily eroding his ability to think freely. Part of him wanted badly to surrender to the muzik, to let his mind go blank, to be meek and filled with a stupid happiness.

He knew that, in a way, he would have to let submission happen — or at least make it *appear* to happen. Any strong or continued free thinking would prevent his release. He would have to fool his captors into thinking he was under the spell of the subliminal messages, while his real self remained free. There was only one way to do this.

He would have to literally divide his mind in two.

He had done it once before, but he didn't know if he could do it again. He'd give it a try. The alternative was death, because Rockson would never allow himself to be complacent Theodore Rockman, living the same controlled life as the other inhabitants of this mad city.

Rockson took a deep breath and focussed on what the Glowers called KA, the inner power that resides within every being, the fount of unlimited psychic energy. He surrounded his inner being with the KA like a plate of iridescent, impervious armor. He projected superficial, conscious thoughts beyond the protection of the KA, out to where the thought police could monitor and the hypno-music could influence.

But his *real* self would be deep, hidden and protected.

Rockson meditated that way for hours, unaware of the passage of time, concentrating until the presence of the KA force would remain in place subconsciously. He hoped.

He came out of his trance ravenous for food. God! When was the last time he had eaten? His hunger threatened to consume him. His rumbling stomach was so empty it practically pressed against his spine.

Rockson had no idea what time it was, whether it was day or night, or how long he had been in the cell. The white glow remained steady from the ceiling. The muzik swirled in lulling waves—but he was immune to the messages within it.

At the conscious thought of food, a slot in the bottom of the cell door opened and a tray slid in. The slot hissed shut.

Rockson couldn't believe his eyes. The tray was heaped with food, all of which smelled and looked exquisitely delicious. There was a huge slab of animal meat, cooked well-done and glistening with marbled fat, and a tuber that looked just like a potato, only it was brown instead of blue. The tuber was split open and covered with a melted yellow substance.

Some of the items he had never seen before—little, wrinkled green pellets sitting in a pile, and a ball of orange-colored fruit that appeared to have a tough, thick skin.

Rockson salivated. He had never been so hungry in his life. The hypno-music invited him to eat, enjoy himself, taste the delicious food. Impulsively he reached out to grab the meat.

Stop! The KA Force commanded within him. *You cannot touch the food! You cannot eat!*

Rockson stopped his hand in midair, then slowly withdrew it from the tray. With overwhelming sadness, he knew he could not eat the food, for it was tainted with tranquilizers and mind-altering drugs—just like most other food he had discovered in the city. Didn't he remember?

Rockson ached. He was nearly faint from hunger, yet he could not touch a single green pellet, or even lick the fat from the meat.

"Damn!" he exclaimed.

The hypno-music changed. Instead of inviting him to eat, the subliminal messages *commanded* him to eat. The desire for the drugged food was stronger, more irresistible than ever.

Rockson countered by retreating to meditation. He

157

was supposed to be docile, and a docile man would eat. He called forth an image in his mind of himself eating the food on the tray. He imagined himself wolfing down the meat, devouring every last morsel, licking the plate and then his fingers.

While he thought about it, he took the plate and shoved its contents into the toilet. The toilet flushed erratically struggling with the meat, but some sort of suction device eventually pulled it in.

Rockson mournfully watched it disappear. He felt that throwing out the food was one of the hardest things he had ever done in his life. But he knew he couldn't dwell on it, or his hunger would weaken him in more ways than one.

He visualized himself as sated and full: happy Rockson, patting his belly, letting out with a resonant belch. He hoped he was right about there not being any cameras in the cell.

Rockson kept track of time according to the meals he was sent. After the first meal, no more food had appeared at his spontaneous thought. Instead, a tray materialized at regular intervals. Like the first time, he imagined himself eating the food with immense enjoyment, while he shoved it down the plumbing.

He estimated that the equivalent of two days had passed, during which he had neither seen another human being nor heard a human voice.

On the second day, while Rockson was lying on his cot trying not to think of food, the door to his cell opened and a tall, robed man entered. He introduced himself: "I'm Bishop Pohsib. How are you, my son?"

he said, smiling down at Rockson. "I heard you are a fan of mine, sneaked into mass to see me."

Rockson restrained himself from jumping up. By now the authorities would expect a dull, submissive man pumped full of drugs and subliminal programming.

He slowly got to his feet. The cot vanished into the wall. "I'm so happy to see you," Rockson said in a slightly dreamy voice. "I'm comfortable, and the food is delicious."

The bishop beamed. "Good. I knew you would be well cared for." His face darkened to a scowl. "The police report on you is not good, Theodore. Dangerous. Free thought. Running from authority. These crimes normally carry heavy punishment."

Rockson didn't have to work to look worried. The bishop went on, "But I told the Chessman I thought your illness was temporary, that you would recover quickly with the proper treatment. Your citizen record has been unblemished your whole life."

"I apologize for my mistakes," said Rockson humbly. "I was under evil influence."

"Apparently so. You responded well to treatment." The robed man smiled again. "Watch me on *TV* from now on, okay?"

Rockson noted that he was armed with a large gun, tucked into a belt in the folds of his robe. It would be so easy to wrest it away from him . . .

It was also a dangerous thought. He summoned up the protective shield of the KA force. If they thought he was "cured," he could get out handily enough.

"Bishop," Rockson began in a plaintive tone with his head slightly bowed, "I miss my wife and family, and my job. I even miss my dog. Can I go home now?"

The man looked pleased. "That's why I'm here, my son. Your family misses you, too. Your wife, Kim, is here, waiting to take you home. The Chessman will allow your release as soon as I report you are cured."

Rockson fell on his knees and grasped the fleshy hand of the bishop. "I am, Your Holiness, I swear I am! I want nothing more than to be a good citizen!" He stifled the gag of disgust that rose in his throat.

"Splendid. Our society needs productive men like you, Theodore Rockman. I will tell the guards you are ready to rejoin the Chessman's happy pawns."

With a beatific smile on his face, Rockson let the bishop escort him out of the cell and into the embrace of clingy little Kim, who warbled and trilled with happiness to be reunited with him. Rockson hoped the hypno-music was loud enough to drown out the rumbling of his empty, hunger-pained stomach.

Outside in the brilliant sunlight, Rockson discovered it was morning rush hour. Kim shoved a briefcase and a garment bag at him.

"Hurry," she urged him. "You have just enough time to make it to the office. You can change there. And I put eight dollars, and your lunch, and your wallet in your briefcase."

Rockson stared stupidly at the briefcase and garment bag and then at Kim. "Work?"

"Yes, you're expected back on the job—*today*. You have to make up for lost time. Hurry! You know it's a sin to be late!"

"But how will I get there?"

"The bus, silly," said Kim impatiently, pointing at

one passing by, loaded with dazed-looking commuters. "The one you always take! Come home early—let's make love again!"

She propelled him to the bus stop and waited until he had jammed himself onto the next crowded vehicle. As the bus lurched away from the curb, he caught a glimpse of Kim waving after him.

Shit, he thought. For all my effort, I'm back to square one! He shrugged. For now, the thing to do was go back to work and pretend he was a mindless office worker. He looked about him. The passengers on the bus all wore the same glazed expression. He peeked through the bodies to look out the window. The pedestrians were stamped with the same vacant bliss.

In the bus and out on the sidewalks, the hypno-music swelled and swirled, subtly reminding everyone of their total obeisance to the Chessman.

As if led by some invisible force, he got off at the appropriate stop and went into the glass skyscraper that housed his office. He rode up the elevator with a dozen glassy-eyed workers, and changed in the twentieth-floor men's room.

Rockson carefully opened the door of his office, intending to slink in as unnoticed as possible—and was greeted by shrieks from his co-workers.

"Hooray! Welcome back, Teddy! Again!" cried Rona, stepping up and throwing her arms around his neck. She was wearing a skin-tight red dress that matched her flaming hair. The dress and the way she rubbed against him left none of her full figure to his imagination.

Rona squealed with delight while the co-workers

hopped and jumped behind her. "Teddy's back! Teddy's back!" they chanted. "Hooray for Teddy!"

Rockson was speechless. But he noticed that behind the glee was a scrutiny, a watchfulness, in the eyes of his co-workers. They were still the Chessman's pawns, and they had been directed, he suspected, to be alert for warning signs of . . . *nonconformity*.

"Did you have a good rest?" asked Rona, wiggling against him.

"Rest? Oh, yes," said Rockson, extricating himself from her grasp. He screwed himself up for his act. "Thank you all for such a wonderful welcome. But we must get to work. It is a sin to be unproductive!" He nearly choked on the words.

"Praise the Chessman for Teddy's recovery!" someone shouted. Others picked it up. "Yes praise the Chessman! Praise the Chessman!"

Rockson walked into his private office. A walnut desk, oiled and shined, was piled with neat stacks of paper awaiting his attention. Rona and the others followed him, clustering in the doorway. There was a sudden tension in the air while everyone watched and waited for him to start work. This was, after all, the *second* time Teddy had been in a scrape with the police.

Shit, thought Rockson, what was it that I do here?

He paused and smiled, hoping everyone would go back to whatever accounting people did. They didn't. They were practically holding their breath in unison.

Rockson set his garment bag and briefcase down on the sofa and walked to the desk. He sat down in the big brown leather chair. He slapped the arms. He looked up at Rona; she was beaming at him, but there was an odd, steely look in her eyes.

He took a paper off the top of one of the stacks. It was filled with rows and columns of numerals. He picked up a number-three pencil and started making scribbles on the papers.

Was he *doomed* to stay in this bizarre city, stuck in time a hundred years earlier than his world, until the nuclear war? The world Rockson came from—the world he called reality—was admittedly savage. But this world was worse. At least, in *his* world, no one controlled his mind—he was free of that ultimate invasion.

Rockson felt a flash of homesickness. He wanted desperately to get away from these mind-controlled robots with their horrible muzik, their thought police . . . He longed for the strontium clouds and the black pits of nuclear-mutated waste. Yes, he would even prefer Streltsy and his KGB thugs over the Chessman and his mind-controlled minions.

He stared absently at the columns of numerals, wondering how much longer he could keep up his charade.

"Is everything all right, Teddy?" asked Rona anxiously.

Then, in a deep corner of his mind, Rockson felt the power of the Glowers. His KA energy reached out to him, protecting him, guiding him. Suddenly he knew what to say. Words tumbled from his lips like automatic speech.

"Rona," he blurted, "where's my coffee? You know I always like it waiting for me. And what have you done with my number-two pencils? You *know* I start the day with three sharp number-twos laid right *here*." He stabbed his finger to a place on his desk, not having the vaguest idea what a number-two pencil was.

A collective sigh of relief rose from Rona and the co-workers. Teddy Rockman had passed their little test. He was cured of deviant behavior at last!

"I'm so sorry, Teddy," cooed Rona. "I was so *excited* about your coming back that I must have forgotten!" She bustled off, her voluptuous hips swaying beneath the tight fabric of her red satin dress.

Rockson leveled a serious gaze at the rest of the office workers. "We're wasting the Chessman's time," he admonished them. To his relief, the spell upon them was indeed broken, and they hurried back to their own jobs.

He swiveled his chair around to the tinted-glass windows, to look out upon the shining city sparkling in the desert sun. In his direct line of sight was the white ultramodern sliver called City Hall Tower. It soared two hundred feet into the air.

Inside it somewhere was Chessman. Rock knew that he stood no chance of escaping this crazy world until he broke the mind-controlling grip of the Chessman. Surely the Chessman had devised the Veil, the force field around the city. And it had to be shut down. And Rockson had to see who was behind that mask he always wore. And why the Chessman's voice was so familiar.

Chapter 13

Rockson somehow managed to get through the day at the office without making revealing slips in behavior or words. The effort created enormous strain; he felt drenched in sweat by the time he escaped to board the bus to go home.

Avoiding drinking the coffee and eating the lunch Kim had prepared proved to be the trickiest acts of all. Rockson watered a spike-leafed palm by the window with the coffee, wishing it happy dreams. He sneaked the lunch into the men's room and flushed it down the john.

On his way home, he was surrounded by thousands of people with the unending glassy-eyed, pacified look. No one was ever out of sight of an armed rookie. Some of the police stood on corners while others strolled the sidewalks. Some sat in glass-walled cages perched high over the streets, where they could keep an eye on traffic and any irregular or sudden movements. With their mirrored glasses and visors, it was difficult to tell what they really were looking at — which no doubt added greatly to their effectiveness, Rockson thought.

He also noticed that the citizens neither acknowledged the police nor seemed afraid of them. The police were simply there, an accepted part of daily life.

"Teddy, darling!" bubbled Kim as he entered his apartment in the middle of the block on Southeast Tenth Street. She hugged him and kissed him primly on the cheek. "I've fixed your favorite dinner—meatloaf!"

He wasn't sure what meatloaf was, but at the thought of food, Rockson's stomach clamored to be fed. He was at a point where he was almost ready to cave in and eat the tranquilized food. He must have grimaced unconsciously, for Kim's happy expression changed to one of anxiety.

"What's the matter, dear—aren't you hungry? You *love* my meatloaf."

Rockson slipped out of her embrace and loosened his tie. This uniform that men wore to work was constricting and uncomfortable. "Uh, as a matter of fact, I, uh, had a big lunch."

Kim's eyes widened. "Big lunch? But, Teddy, I didn't pack that much. You never like big lunches."

"Well, er, everyone in the office wanted to celebrate, and . . ."

"I see," said Kim, nodding knowingly. "So they brought in food and you had a banquet."

"Yes," said Rockson uncertainly, hoping that was the right answer.

Apparently it wasn't. "How did you get permission?" Kim asked.

"Permission?"

"Why, Teddy, you *know* you can't hold a celebration without authorization from the Chessman." She gave him a steely look.

Rockson shrugged. "Then, obviously, someone got it."

"But how would they know in advance that you would be back to work *today*? It takes time to get an authorization, and it's only good for twenty-four hours. Even *I* didn't know you were getting out until this morning."

Rockson was saved from Kim's interrogation by the entrance of his two children, who came running into the apartment pell-mell.

"Daddy, Daddy!" they shrieked, jumping up and down around him. "Daddy, will you come out and play with us?"

Kim shooed Teddy junior and Barbara away. "Daddy just got home from work and is tired. Go clean up for dinner."

"What's for dinner, Mom?" asked Teddy junior.

"Meatloaf, darling."

"Yay!" The children streaked off toward the TV.

Rockson thought, I can't take any more of this. I've got to get out of here—this place is nuts!

After dinner, both the little blond devils went to their rooms.

Then she and Rockson settled down to spend the evening glued to the fake Spanish Oak console Motorola, watching dramas about virtuous people overcoming evil—the evil being in the form of degenerate homeless men preying on saintly kids—or sitcoms about couples buying their first condominium apartments and discovering their interesting neighbors.

After several of these programs—at which point

167

Rockson was ready to run screaming from the house — Bishop Pohsib took over the airwaves and launched into an evangelical sermon about "playing by the rules of life."

Kim, a beatific look upon her face, turned to Rockson and purred, "I suppose, Teddy, we really *ought* to have another child. The Chessman says three is minimum, and four is ideal."

Rockson felt the hair on the back of his neck stand on end. "Perhaps so, sweetie," he mumbled. The "sweetie" came out awkwardly. Kim had already reproached him for not being liberal with her favorite nickname.

Despite her suggestion for enlarging the family, Rockson easily managed to avoid having sex with her, or even kissing her in any passionate way. Not that he would have minded — not in the least. He was still red-blooded in *that* department. But he was afraid that the release of sexual energy might jeopardize his thin margin of control with the KA force, which kept his mind clear.

So, he had pleaded fatigue, and she didn't seem to be upset. In fact, much to his confusion, she seemed almost relieved, and curled up into a tight ball on her side of the bed, with her back to him. She was asleep in minutes. She was not like the real Kim at all — *his* Kim, back in Century City.

Rockson couldn't get to sleep, and had to keep his empty stomach in constant check. One audible rumble, and he feared Kim would leap out of bed and run to the kitchen to fix him a cold meatloaf sandwich.

Skippy, the family dog, grumbled and sighed in sleep at the foot of the bed. A red oaf of a thing —

and not any breed that Rockson recognize—Skippy had treated him disdainfully all evening, much to Kim's consternation. Rock knew animals had a powerful sixth sense, and he hoped Skippy would not betray him.

Rockson stared into the darkness, one arm crooked behind his head. He felt helpless, stuck in this time-warp rut, like a slave chained by the neck to a milling wheel. He couldn't take it another minute. He would have to act now, while no one suspected him of free will, before he committed an error that would send him back to "detention and rehabilitation." There would be no more chances from the Chessman.

Rockson slowly rose up in the bed and shifted his legs out from under the covers. The mattress creaked at the redistribution of his weight. The dog moaned and changed position. Rock put his feet on the floor and carefully stood up, trying not to awaken Kim.

He was so dizzy that even the slow movement made him violently dizzy. He swayed and flung out his hand in an effort to recover his balance. He hit the ceramic table-lamp by the side of the bed. It tipped over into the wall. The dog sprang to his feet with a growl.

Kim sat bolt upright with a gasp. Then she exhaled in relief. "Oh, Teddy, it's you. I thought a homeless had broken in . . ." She threw off the covers. The bedroom was not completely dark, and Rockson could make out her features. She had an efficient look he did not like.

"What's the matter, darling sweetie pie?" Kim said. Before Rockson could answer, she went on, "You're hungry, I'll bet. Come, I'll make you a meatloaf sandwich." She started to climb out of bed, but Rockson protested.

"No! I mean, don't please. I'm not hungry—really."

"How could you not be hungry, dearie? You didn't eat or drink a thing all evening. It's not like you. You always have a big glass of Tranqua-milk before going to sleep. Are you sure you're all right?"

"I'm fine, ah, sweetie. Just couldn't drop off, I guess."

Kim got up, her sexy white nightgown flowing after her. The real Kim would have loved such a sheer, seductive piece of clothing. She could have been Venus herself.

She switched on the lamp on her side of the bed. "You wait right there. I'll get you a nice big glass of Tranqua-milk. You see, Teddy, you shouldn't try to break habits, especially ones that are good for you."

Rockson could tell that further protest would be futile. The "little woman," as she liked to call herself, was as determined as the most unruly 'brid when she had her mind set on something. He'd learned *that* lesson in a hurry.

Humming, Kim floated out of the bedroom. Rockson heard her rummaging through the refrigerator in the kitchen down the hall. He sat down on the edge of the bed with a sigh. The dog licked his hands. It was the first sign of friendliness the animal had shown. Or was it commiseration?

Kim returned bearing two huge glasses of an ugly, blue-white liquid. "I thought I could use some myself," she said, handing one of the glasses to Rockson. "It's been one exciting day--the TV programs were *so* good!"

Rockson reluctantly took the glass. "You shouldn't have gone to the trouble," he mumbled.

"No trouble. Drink up, darling. Cheers!" Kim tilted her head back and drained half the glass in one long pull. Damn, thought Rockson, she'd be a hell of a drinker where he came from.

Kim swallowed and looked at Rockson. "Well — aren't you going to drink it?"

Rockson hesitated. A glass of Tranqua-milk was just what he didn't need.

"Theodore Rockman, what's the matter with you? I'm beginning to think the bishop might have let you out a little too soon."

At those words, Rockson felt a stab of fear. He forced himself to smile as disarmingly as possible. "Nothing's wrong, sweetie," he said in a light tone. "Why, I was just reflecting on how lucky a man I am to have you to take care of me."

Kim beamed. "Teddy, you're so sweet!" She took another gulp of Tranqua-milk, watching him at the same time.

Rockson could see no way out. To not drink the milk would tip off Kim that he was not "recovered" after all.

He smiled and took a huge gulp, filling his mouth with the blue-white liquid. He'd expected it to taste bad, but it had a pleasant, sweetish taste. Of course — the Chessman would want everyone to drink up without a flinch.

The Tranqua-milk reminded him of honey. He'd been privileged to taste honey once, from the Sacred Beehive kept under constant guard in one of the Free

171

Cities. Honeybees had been nearly wiped out by nuclear fallout from the war. Luckily a hive had been preserved, and a mutated strain could withstand low levels of radiation. There was great hope among Americans that eventually there would be enough honeybees to set some of them loose upon the terrain.

But that was in another world. And Rockson was here, in this whacky world, on the verge of tranquilizing himself into oblivion.

He faked a swallow and patted his stomach, then got up and headed for the bathroom. As soon as he got the door closed, he turned on the faucet and spit the Tranqua-milk into the toilet. He waited several minutes and then flushed. At the basin he splashed water on his face, and returned to the bedroom. He hoped the Tranqua-milk hadn't been in his mouth long enough for his tissue to absorb a significant amount of the drug.

As Rockson hoped, Kim had finished her milk, turned off the light, and tucked herself back under the covers. She was already drowsy. "Don't forget to finish your milk," she said in a thick, sleepy voice.

"I think I'll just relax and sip on it for a while," Rockson lied.

"G'night, darling." Kim was asleep by the time the words were out of her mouth.

Rockson breathed out a sigh. *Thank God*—I'm getting out of here.

He ripped off his cotton pajamas. He had loathed them from the minute Kim had gotten them out of a drawer and placed them on his side of the bed with a loving pat. They were white baggy things with little maroon paisleys on them. They looked like something

President Zhabnov would have worn on a bad night.

The more Rockson saw of how men lived in this bizarre place and time, the more desperate he was to get back to his own continuum. Here men were milksops, and women little more than shoppers—and bed companions—though this Kim was good at the latter!

Quietly and slowly, Rockson got dressed. He put on a shirt and a pair of comfortable pants that Kim had called "Calvin's." He had figured out an excuse for stepping out.

The dog watched him with great interest. When Rockson finished putting on socks and sneakers, a whimper escaped from low in the dog's throat.

"Friend? Don't worry, Skippy, I'm not leaving you behind," Rockson whispered. "There's an old saying that dog is man's best friend, and while you don't look like any dog I've ever seen, I'm sure you live up to that, just the same." The whisper seemed to quiet the scraggly mop of a dog.

In the kitchen utility closet, Rockson found Skippy's leash. As soon as the dog discovered he was going to be taken on a walk, he became excited and did a nervous jig on the kitchen linoleum. The disdain was gone—he was Rock's best friend. Rockson, afraid the dog would bark or make too much noise, quickly shooed him outside.

The night air was cool and dry. The sky above Rockson was a canopy of black filled with thousands upon thousands of stars. A breeze blowing was fresh and crisp. The whole scene had a serenity that Rockson found quite pleasing and soothing. Even on star-filled nights in his own world, there was still a turbulence, either in the air currents or in the clouds one could see flickering in the upper atmosphere.

The only thing marring the setting was the infernal mind muzik. It was pumped everywhere, around the clock—there was no escape.

"C'mon, boy." Rockson clicked his tongue at the dog, which set off on a happy trot.

He quickly saw that the dog was not going to work. He'd hoped Skippy would provide him cover if they encountered thought police. When Skippy was no longer necessary, Rockson planned to turn him loose.

But the dog wanted less to walk and more to lunge after every cat and other night creature that skulked about in the shadows.

Rockson unhooked the leash and slapped the dog on the rump. "Beat it," he commanded. Skippy dashed off into the darkened streets.

Rockson stuffed his hands in his pockets and strolled on, heading toward the city center. He seemed to be the only human up and about.

Not quite.

"You there." The deep, authoritative voice behind him startled him. Turning, Rockson was confronted by a policeman. The uniform of the night patrol was slightly different than that of the day cops. Instead of a mirrored visor, this officer wore infrared night-vision goggles. He had his heavy nightstick tucked casually in the crook of his right arm. Rock also noticed the back tank and flamethrower.

"Identify yourself," the officer commanded, approaching Rockson.

Rockson stood still. "Theodore Rockman."

"That's not proper identification." The officer's

mouth was set in a hard line.

His name not a proper ID? Rockson thought fast. Everyone must be assigned a number or code—it would make sense in this controlled society. But what was *his*? He didn't know.

"I live near here," he said evasively. "I couldn't sleep, so I thought I'd take a little walk. It's a pleasant night, isn't it?"

The officer didn't respond. With his grim mouth and opaque goggles, it was impossible to tell what he was thinking.

The policeman put a hand to his ear. Rockson guessed he was wearing a micro-headset. He had turned a small knob.

"Your voice print has been identified," said the officer. "Theodore Rockman, Number Two-Nine-Zero-Five-Seven, District Thirty-six."

Rockson immediately committed the ID to memory. It could save his life.

The officer continued, "You were released from detention today. Treatment for violence, noncomformist behavior, and free thought." He stepped closer, peering at Rockson through his infrared goggles. "State your business. Why are you out at this hour?"

The cop had instantly found his record—a link with a computer? Rockson wondered what else was being instantly analyzed. His stomach was a tight ball of tension. If he got thrown in the clink again . . . Maybe he could say he was walking the dog and it had run away. *No*. It's probably illegal to walk the dog without a damned leash. And even small infractions had heavy penalties.

"The purpose of your nocturnal activity?" snapped

175

the officer.

Rockson stammered. "I — I said, I couldn't sleep. I thought a walk would be relaxing — you know, after being in rehabilitation . . ." His voice trailed off. This was sounding stupid. Shit! Why couldn't he think of something brilliant to say? Then he did think of an excuse.

"Bishop Pohsib said to take walks if I couldn't sleep," Rockson blurted. "He said it would help."

The officer hesitated. He cocked his head, listening to his headset. "You were released by Bishop Pohsib . . ."

"It's true," insisted Rockson. "It's part of my treatment. I have to walk. Lots."

The officer hesitated again, listening to the device in his ear. "Okay, you're cleared. But keep the walk short, Two-Nine-Zero-Five-Seven. A five-block radius from the house in all directions. And tell your wife to buy number-one strength Tranqua-milk next time." He pivoted sharply on his heel and marched away.

Rockson sighed. He waited until the officer was out of sight, then he slipped into the shadows. He could afford no more run-ins with the thought police.

He continued toward the center city, avoiding detection by at least a dozen rookies along the way. The city was under their watchful eye all night, he surmised.

In the commercial zone, Rockson passed by the window of a gun store. An iron gate was pulled across the front. A sign informed anyone who was curious that the store was for "authorized state personnel only," meaning the thought police, holy priests, and others of the Chessman's violent circle. Another sign warned that the iron gate was electrified. Maybe that was a new policy, because of his break-ins.

And, to further discourage temptation, a camera was positioned prominently to film anyone caught lingering over the display of weapons in the window. Apparently the authorities didn't want unauthorized pawns looking at weapons long enough to want one.

Out of camera range and hidden in the shadows, Rockson studied the storefront. He needed a weapon—a super-weapon like the compound gun he had put together before his capture—but getting one seemed remote. This gun shop was burglar-proof. Maybe he should jump a rookie. But their pistols were junk—twelve-shot Tokarovs. And weed-burners were unwieldy—and not his style. He moved one. The entire area around the gun store was well bugged with sensors to detect a lingering presence. Infrared micro-cams, microphones, the works.

Further in toward the city center, he passed what looked like a lump of filthy rags heaped on top of a grate that vented the underground rail transportation to the sidewalk above. Such debris was unusual in the Chessman's spotless city, at least anywhere near the tall condominiums.

Then Rockson realized it wasn't debris at all, but a man dressed in rags and huddled on the grate in sleep. It surprised him, the number of derelicts that were tolerated in the rigid discipline of the Chessman. With police everywhere, the homeless had learned how to look like part of the scene, invisible people. Piles of nothing.

Rockson didn't disturb the sleeping man. Perhaps

this derelict was really an auxiliary of the police—an unsuspected sentry or spy. Rockson hurried on.

Soon he was standing at the perimeter of City Hall Square, gazing up at the icy-white spire of the tower that jutted into the night sky. The tower itself was protected by a high brick wall laced with electrical sensor wires. Sentries marched back and forth on a parapet on the other side of the wall, and stood guard in boxes at the corners.

The grounds also were protected by radar—Rockson spotted the dish antennae. A battery of laser spotlights ringed the wall around the tower, their lights now dead, but ready to turn into blinding beams if a warning was sounded.

Inside, the grounds were brightly lit, judging from the glow that rose over the walls. The compound had an evil look, and a chill ran down his spine.

The muzik was particularly strong there, and Rockson had to take a moment to reinforce his resistance powers against its insidious, hypnotizing effects.

Armed guards patrolled the streets around the compound. The Chessman took no chances, despite the tranquilizing and programming of the population.

Rockson gritted his teeth. Somehow he would get past the radar and the armed guards, avoid the laser spotlights—and climb the tower of Chessman. One man against hundreds. One unarmed man against an super arsenal of weapons. *Who* was he kidding?

Suddenly Rockson's concentration was broken. He held his breath. What was that noise? A footstep? He whirled, peering into the darkness around him, hearing raspy breathing. His eyes searched the area for the source.

A low voice came out of the night. "Hey, you, citizen. What do you think you're doing here?"

Rockson spotted the owner of the voice. It was a man, short, squat, and hunched over, his face covered with greasy dirt, his body clothed in soiled, torn rags. It was the derelict he'd observed sleeping on the grate—the *same* derelict he'd met at the city dump. Barrelman.

Chapter 14

"Get out of the light," the derelict hissed at Rockson. "They'll get you!"

Rockson didn't move. He stood his ground, not certain whether Barrelman was trying to help him or trap him. After all, Barrelman had suggested the crypt as a place to hide.

"Get over here into the bushes! Quick!" The man waved wildly at him, motioning him to approach.

Rockson hesitated, ready to exit at the slightest hint of trouble. He couldn't tell if Barrelman was armed.

"Dammit, get over here!" the man hissed more loudly. "You've been standing in that spot too long! A few more seconds, the heat sensors will notice you!" He added, "I can *help* you!"

Rockson walked toward Barrelman, keeping to the shadows, still wary of a trap. The derelict watched him anxiously, his eyes wide. *"Hurry!"* he urged.

When Rockson reached the inky shadows and the cover of the bushes, the man reached out to grab his sleeve. Rockson pulled back. "What are you doing here?" Rock demanded in a low voice. "Did you know I was found in the crypt?"

"Never mind that now," said the bum, grabbing at Rockson's sleeve again and yanking him down toward the ground. "Get down! You're standing right in the middle of the sensor sweep zone, and if they spot you, we'll both be dead!"

Rockson ducked down into a crouch. Barrelman began pulling on him as he crept through the bushes, away from Tower Square. "We've got to get out of here," he told Rock. "We're pushing our luck as it is."

"Wait a minute," Rockson said, resisting. "To where?"

The man turned to fix Rockson with an impatient expression. "Look, you've got to trust me. I'll tell you when we're safe. If you don't believe me, then go ahead and take your chances with *them*." He motioned toward the square with its squads of guards and thought police, then jabbed a thumb at himself. "I've seen your bravery and come to offer my help." He turned and began rustling through the bushes, half on his hands and knees, half in a crouch-walk.

Rockson followed. One thing he didn't have was allies. If this shabbily dressed man was on the level, then Rockson would no longer be alone. He'd take any improvement in the odds that he could get.

The derelict led Rockson through a dark, quiet park, keeping to the shrubbery. Presently they faced a deserted downtown street. Barrelman paused until he was certain there were no policemen around, then did a crablike scuttle to a drainage grate in the street, near the sidewalk.

He lifted the grate and waved at Rockson to come forward. He slid into the manhole and motioned for Rockson to come and do the same.

Rockson slipped down into a chilly, dark, damp tube. It was made of steel, with small ladder rungs welded into its side. He replaced the grate with care, fitting it into its notches in the street, then scrambled down after the derelict.

The tube led to the city sewer system—it was obvious from the rank odor that grew stronger the deeper they went. They descended lower and lower, Barrelman moving swiftly, at home in this environment. Rockson had to work to keep up with him.

A tiny, dim spot of light appeared at their feet and grew larger, but not much brighter. The light opened out into a web of interconnecting tunnels. Rockson and the derelict dropped onto the floor of the largest tunnel with a splash. A few inches of foul-smelling water sat in the bottom of the tube. Rockson stamped his soaked shoes and planted his feet higher in the tube, above the waterline, on a narrow walkway.

The tunnels were lit by bare bulbs connected to strands of wire. The lights didn't appear to be part of the original design, but crudely added by hand.

"One of our own touches," Barrelman said proudly, pointing to the lights. "They're electrical, of course—dangerous with all this water. But what the hell, the view is nice when you fall off the Board of Life—they say."

Rockson wondered who the collective "our" was. Did the sewer system hold some subterranean population? He didn't have the chance to ask, for his guide was already moving swiftly ahead of him.

"This way," said Barrelman, ducking down one of the tunnels to his left. He avoided the trickle of water by straddling it and walking along the curved sides of the tunnel. Rockson followed suit.

Gradually, Rockson began to realize the enormity of the plumbing system they were in. It was a maze of tunnels and tubes, some dry, some partially filled with water; some lit by the bare light bulbs, some dark. Overhead and along the sides of the tunnels ran pipes of varying sizes. The system was filled with rumbling and rushing noises—the sound of water flowing and unseen machinery in motion.

One noise he *didn't* hear was the hypno-music.

"Does this stretch under the entire city?" he called out to the derelict. His words reverberated through the tunnel.

Barrelman stopped and turned. "Yes," he answered in a whisper. "The catacombs cover one hundred and eighty square kilometers. Don't talk again, until I give the signal that it's okay—there are too many vibrations from the echoes here that could be heard on the surface."

Rockson nodded and they set off again. The man led him on a confusing path of connecting tunnels. None were marked; how could he possibly know where he was going? What was worse was how Rockson would ever get out on his own, if the need arose. He could wander forever in the maze of sewers, a trapped rat.

The man dodged suddenly to his right. Rockson followed, and they burst into a cavernous room lit by more strung bulbs. There were people in the room— about a dozen, he guessed—and they all stopped what they were doing and stared at him in silence, eyes wide with uncertainty. There were both men and women in the group, all dressed in the same dirty rags as his guide.

Barrelman slipped behind Rockson and pushed shut a door, the only opening to the cavern. Rockson distinctly did not like being shut in a room with only one way out—even if he was among people who claimed to be friendly.

The man heaved out a great sigh. He stepped forward and indicated Rockson with a grand flourish. "Friends," he said, "Here is our free-thoughter!"

The uncertain faces broke into tentative smiles; murmurs arose. "You're accepted," said Barrelman, "as a recruit."

Rockson narrowed his eyes at the man. "A recruit for what?"

The man took off his ragged jacket and threw it in a pile of rags. "It will all be explained. We can talk freely here. As you can see"—he pointed to the walls and ceiling of the room—"we have padded the interior to dampen sound vibration. This was once a storage area. But someone began dumping defective plumbing equipment in here, and the room eventually was abandoned, along with the junk." He pointed to the dim back of the cavern, where Rockson could make out the glint of metal.

"So relax, my friend," said the man. "You *are* among friends here. None of us are the Chessman's damned pawns."

A few of the others shifted position on the floor of the cavern to make room for Rockson to sit down. They had been busy with handiwork, sewing, repairing odd-looking objects, fashioning things. Rockson hesitantly took the proffered seat and lowered himself onto a couple of cushions. Some of the tension flowed out of him.

"As you know, my name is Barrelman," said the man who had led Rockson to the underground. "It was Roger Barrelman, when I was a citizen. Now it's just Barrelman. We all have only one name here—it keeps things simple."

"That's nice." Rockson wasn't sure he wanted to try explaining who *he* really was. Or thought he was. If it came to that, there would be the right time. "Call me Rock."

Barrelman grinned. "Okay, Rock. I used to be a pawn, just like you. Lost my job as a shopkeeper when the shut-down came."

"Maybe you'd better start at the beginning," said Rockson, not wanting to get into a discussion about the dreadfully boring work of accountants. "I have a feeling there's a hell of an explanation coming."

"Indeed," said Barrelman. "Would you like some cold cuts and a drink while I talk? You must be famished."

Rockson smiled. "As long as it's not drugged."

"No, of course not. Only the fresh food is—preservatives destroy the Chessman's control drug."

Barrelman dug around in a little picnic chest and found a sandwich wrapped in a plastic bag, handed it to Rockson. "Okay?"

"*Anything*, man, anything. I'm starved." Rockson let go of the KA-control of his hunger and devoured the sandwich.

"But how do you get it?" he asked when he finished.

"From the garbage behind the condos—the big trash bins. They waste a lot of stuff. They like

185

asparagus sprouts and chickpeas, and that sort of thing. Most of the sandwiches only have a bite or two out of them."

Rockson hesitated, then asked for another sandwich. What the hell—he was wearing cast-offs, he might as well eat "previously eaten" food.

Barrelman even found some flat soda pop for him. Lemon-lime.

Barrelman sat down on a dirty, lumpy pillow opposite Rockson. By now, others in the cavern had returned to their individual tasks. "I'll begin at the beginning, as you suggested. We are the Resistance Underground Network—we call ourselves Runners. It's an especially appropriate name, since we're always running from the Chessman's militia. Didn't mention it before, because I didn't quite trust you."

"We got our start when our Founder discovered that after skipping several meals due to illness, he had broken the spell of the drugs. He also found that without the drugged food, it was possible to resist the hypno-music."

A woman called Rosa set down two large tumblers of a clear golden liquid in front of Barrelman and Rockson.

"Apple juice," said Barrelman. "We stole it from the deli near Temple Square. We let it sit long enough for the drug to diminish." He took a big gulp. "Try some."

Rockson did. Somehow his instincts told him Barrelman could be trusted. He spoke the truth. The apple juice tasted exquisite. It whetted his appetite, making his stomach clamor for solid food. He drank the entire glass, and as soon as he put the empty tumbler down, Rosa refilled it.

"More food is coming," she said.

Barrelman continued. "He had a strong mind, the Founder. He liked having free thoughts and didn't want to resume a controlled life."

"How did he avoid the thought police?" asked Rockson.

"He found, by trial and error, that aberrant but harmless behavior was tolerated. The Chessman seems to realize that a certain percentage of the population will not conform to guidelines. Noncomformists who threaten his control are dealt with swiftly. But we, the homeless, ugly wretches who sleep in doorways, we are often left alone, or merely chased. You see, we act as a warning to the other citizens, a warning to Chessman's controlled pawns. They are afraid they will become like us if they don't conform, follow orders."

"I see."

Barrelman finished his apple juice. "The Founder had a keen eye for spotting others who were on the edge, so to speak. He recruited us over a period of time. There are several hundred of us, scattered throughout the sewers. The rookies call us "the duct people," think we never come up."

"You speak of the Founder in the past tense. Who was he? What happened to him?"

Barrelman cast his eyes down. "He was an unusual man; his name isn't important. He was picked up and devoured by a brush-eater while sleeping on a grate. It was no accident. The authorities had spotted him as a ringleader. Alas, we have only hope to maintain us, now that he is gone. Though he did predict—"

Rosa returned, holding a hubcap of an automobile. The concave side was piled with scraps of food. She handed it to Rockson saying, "It's a bit stale."

"Don't apologize," Rock said, eagerly taking the plate. "You don't know how grateful I am." He dug into the food with his fingers and began stuffing it in his mouth. He tried now to temper his ravenous appetite. He didn't want cramps.

"Anyway," said Barrelman, "I'm in charge of the Runners now. We live down here in the sewer, but each of us takes turns rotating to the surface."

"How did you find me?"

"Easy. Echoes from the surface. You walk like a cat. Unusual. By the way, all arrests and punishments are publicized—it's a way of maintaining control. Because of your previous record as a fine citizen, you were given rehabilitation instead of annihilation. I had hoped they wouldn't kill you. I knew you had the potential to be one of us. We help you—you help us."

Rockson swallowed. "We have to get out of this city. You don't understand the situation." He debated telling them the truth: that the city was—the world— was on the brink of the nuclear world war. Then he decided not to. Not yet. They might not believe him.

Rockson instead took the psychological approach. "Barrelman, don't you want to be free? Don't you want to roam the country—get out of the city, smell fresh air, seek new opportunity? Chessman does not control the whole world, you know."

"To be free, to be away from the city, is a dream. We roam freely underground, *that* is freedom. We have the entire duct system memorized."

Rock set down the food. He had vacuumed up

everything. "Barrelman, you don't have to live like this. I told you before—you don't have to live like *rats*. Storm the condos above, take what's yours! You know there's no hope, no future, as long as the Chessman is alive. But if he dies . . ."

Barrelman shook his head violently. "You don't know what you're saying. Killing the Chessman is impossible. He is in City Hall Tower, and it is impenetrable. To try to breach it is certain death. Look what happened when you tried to penetrate the Tabernacle."

Rockson fixed Barrelman with an unwavering gaze of his mismatched violet and aquamarine eyes. "You don't know me," he said quickly. "I'm going to get the Chessman. Will the Runners help, or will I do it alone?"

Barrelman was lost in thought for a moment. "It's true that your efforts so far are admirable. Perhaps . . . some of us *might* be willing to follow you in an assault against the Tower." Heads nodded.

The other Runners in the cavern murmured approval. Rosa said, "Let's do it. I'm sick of this life." The leader cast his eyes about the group, looking for negative comments, then returned Rockson's gaze when none materialized.

"We sense in you a strength and determination that is most uncommon for a Salt Lake City citizen," Barrelman said. "I know of no possible explanation, except one . . . The Founder predicted the "White King" would come someday and liberate the city. Are you—you—*the One* we have waited for?"

Rockson boldly seized the opportunity. "I am."

Barrelman bowed his head in a subservient gesture.

189

"Then, we are at your service." They all bowed low.

"Stand up, please. Do you know how we can get arms?"

"No problem," the leader said, getting up. "We have weapons."

"You do?" This was more than Rockson had hoped for.

"I'll show you." Barrelman got up and led Rockson to a connecting antechamber. In the glow of the bare bulbs, Barrelman pointed. Rockson was disheartened to see a pile of crudely fashioned weapons. They were suitable for hand-to-hand fighting, but were no match for the sophisticated artillery of the Chessman's police. Sharpened broomsticks, jagged glass "knives."

"These aren't good for much more than fending off angry dogs," said Rockson with a trace of bitterness in his voice. For a few moments, his glimmer of hope had brightened to a flame, only to be extinguished. What he needed was another super-weapon.

"This is all we have," Barrelman looked sad.

"But you must know where police weapons are stored. You're up on the surface enough."

Barrelman nodded. "It's true. We have quite a spy network. We know where *everything* is in the city."

Rockson grabbed Barrelman by the shoulders and shook him. "For God's sakes, why didn't you *tell* me?"

Barrelman stuttered, but Rockson cut him off. "Never mind. Just tell me where to find *real* weapons."

"If we steal them, they'll be missed. A search will be called."

"By the time anyone knows they're gone," said Rockson, "it won't matter. Listen, I left a very *special* gun in the crypt in the Tabernacle. Can your men up there get it for me unobserved?"

Barrelman said, "Darryl once worked as a janitor there. He can get it for you. I know the gun is powerful, but can you really—Can *we* really defeat the Chessman?"

"Didn't the Founder tell you to trust the White King who came to set the city free?"

Barrelman nodded solemnly. He ordered Darryl to fetch Rockson's compound gun. Rockson took a measure of this man Darryl. He was a trusted aide of the Barrelman, a small fast man with strong, steady brown eyes. He might pull it off. Darryl left on the run, saying, "I'll get it, don't worry."

"Now," Rockson ordered, "let's get you *all* guns." Barrelman, Rockson, and three other Runners wound their way through the smelly sewer system. The air warmed as they traveled, turning the chilly dampness into a cloying, humid heat. They gathered more recruits as they walked, as the news spread of the advent of the "White King" at last. It was hot, but Barrelman seemed immune to the heat and the smell. A life as a garbage-scrounging derelict, living in the sewers, was a life that immunized you to petty annoyances.

About seventy-five of the Runners had pledged their support for an assault on the Tower. All of them had to be properly armed if they were to stand a chance against the Chessman's militia.

Barrelman stopped beneath a skinny tube similar to the one he and Rockson had descended from the street level. "The arsenal is above," he said. "We cannot talk loudly here."

"We will all pass weapons and ammunition down to one another—a human chain," whispered Rockson.

After a brief ascent, they reached a small grating in the cement floor of a dark room. The spill-hole was barely big enough for the average man to squeeze through, but Barrelman, despite his stocky bulk, managed. Water trickled past them.

Rockson crawled up second. He heard Barrelman moving softly about the room, low scrapes punctuating the silence. Then Barrelman began handing him cold metallic objects and wooden boxes. Rock took all he could hold and then climbed down to deposit the goods into waiting hands, then returned for more.

He made at least a dozen trips up and down the arsenal until he was satisfied. He could hardly see, but he knew the feel of submachine guns and ammo boxes.

When they reached the bottom of the tube, Barrelman sighed. "That was all I could risk taking from one place at one time," he explained. "Hopefully, the loss won't be noticed when the morning guard shift comes on—they always check the arsenal. They might not notice until inventory—which, if we're successful, will never happen."

"We'll be successful," Rockson vowed.

"There are several other depots that we know of," Barrelman said.

"Forget it," Rock said. "Everyone: the assault team will assemble in the headquarters cavern."

The men loaded up their booty and carried it back to the cavern headquarters of the Runners. There

192

Rockson spread everything out and examined the pieces. Some of the weapons seemed crude compared to those he was familiar with in his "real" life. He recognized some as M16s and a few AK47s—crude, but they'd do.

Then Darryl came running in a crouch down the long pipe. "I got it. I got Rockson's weapon from the crypt!"

Indeed he had. Rockson thanked Darryl profusely and fondled the compound gun.

Then he put it aside—for the moment. Rockson snapped a magazine into each regular submachine gun and handed them out.

Barrelman looked on in amazement. "A C.P.A. wouldn't know so much about weapons—you truly are 'the White King'!"

Rockson shrugged. "You said it, citizen. I'm the one." He examined the firing pin. "There isn't enough time—or necessity—for everyone to have a compound gun like mine. I'm sorry, but the rest of you will have to do with conventional weapons."

"They'll be enough. I feel braver by the minute!!"

Runners loaded clips into the submachine guns as Rock instructed. In a few minutes Rock taught them the bare rudiments of firing them.

The Runners babbled in a mixture of excitement and apprehension. No one in the history of the Holy Regime had ever attempted a revolution. And who would suspect the lowly bag people of plotting such a crime? Success would bring complete freedom for everyone in Salt Lake City. Failure, they knew, would doom the Runners to torture that was worse than death, and punishment to the innocent, tranquilized citizens as a "lesson." There was a great deal at stake.

The Runners outfitted themselves with their stolen goods. Besides guns, bullets, and a few grenades, they had a few stolen flak jackets and close-fitting helmets made out of a high-impact, heavy plastic. One small crate had held fifty good chronometers—military watches with sweep second hands. Every other Runner—and Rockson—got one and all were synchronized to Barrelman's Seiko. Each jacket and helmet, Rock noticed, bore the insignia of a chess rook. That wasn't a very high rank. Rock wished they had some blue blazers and insignias of the consultants.

"First of all," he said to Barrelman, "we need a map of the Tower compound, and its defenses—do you have such a thing?"

"You bet. We have the very blueprints—stolen from the basement of the city planning office. The founder said to prepare for the day the White King cometh. He said to prepare weapons and secure the plans to the Tower. You didn't like our weapons, but I think you will like these drawings." Barrelman snapped his fingers, and the omnipresent Darryl rushed away with his long, loping, stooped-over gait down the duct. In less than five minutes he came back with rolls of blueprints, some a bit dog-eared and brittle.

Rockson laid them out on the table. Perfect. Only it didn't look like there was any chance of breaching the defenses.

There were three heavy steel-alloy doors inside the main entrance to the Tower, probably heavily guarded. Three checkpoints, where an army of

Freefighters might bog down, let alone a make-do army of derelicts. According to the specifications of the sliding steel doors, not even RPGs or a tank shell could penetrate them. Ditto for the Tower itself, a triple-reinforced marvel of strength.

Rockson sighed. As for a lone infiltrator bluffing his way through the three doors, without the proper codes, without the proper fingerprints—for there were fingerprint-verification locks on all the check-point doors—it was impossible.

Rockson was open to suggestions.

Darryl piped in, "Why can't we fire some of those RPGs right into Chessman's window?—the window at the top of the tower? Why assault the tower at all? Just blast the shit out of the window. The Chessman is always in that room, operating his equipment—whatever that is—and enjoying the overlook. Why do you have to get in the Tower at all?"

Rockson thanked Darryl for his suggestion, and said, "I have to make sure he's dead. We don't even know if that window at the tower-top is breakable. The plans say it's an ordinary stained-glass window, but I think it might have been reinforced."

"He's been seen at the open window," said Rosa. "He stands there sometimes, in his mask, he does. Looking out over his city. It's a window, all right."

"Did you see him?"

She shook her head, "Not I, but the Professor, my old friend, now dead. He was a wise one. He watched the Tower, sometimes, through some old field glasses he had. He was always studying, figuring things. He was a great man. . . ." She looked down sadly. "He died, saving me and my friends."

No one else had ever seen the Chessman in the window. But Rockson believed Rosa's story. "Well, assuming it's a window, and that Chessman is there in the Tower, I still want to confront him personally. I have to know the secret of the Veil, how to turn it off. I have to know who the Chessman is. I know his voice from somewhere. And most of all, I must be sure he's killed — I will kill him myself." A glow came into the eyes of the Doomsday Warrior. "And I think I know how to get to him.

"First we must get into the compound. Besides the wall and the guards, there are the elaborate detectors to knock out.

"You and your people will use your greatest talent — stealth. It won't be a frontal assault — we will garrote the guards, cut the detectors first — you know where the electric cables are?"

Barrelman nodded. "They are aboveground — except for a short segment that runs underground. There's no way to kill the circuit — there are backup systems all over. The Chessman takes no shortcuts when it comes to his security."

"Maybe you can't kill it, but could you interrupt it? A few seconds, a minute, and I can get past it."

Barrelman thought about it for a moment. "I think we could do that, yes. We know where the circuit breakers are. It would have to be precisely timed, of course. And you would have to move *very* fast."

"Just take care of your end of the business," Rockson said, "and I will get to the Tower."

"How do you plan to *enter* the Tower?"

"By climbing it. The greatest talent a Coloradan has is climbing. I've scaled peaks that make the tower look like a toothpick. Admittedly, I had good equipment. Pitons, rope—and there had been some handholds. But I can do it."

"And if something goes wrong—what about escape?"

Rockson's face was hard as steel. "Nothing will go wrong, Barrelman." He let the words sink in, then went on. "Now, you must tell me everything you know that isn't spelled out on the drawings. How many guards. Where they're positioned."

Barrelman pointed to the places on the blueprints that were fortified pillboxes. Four corners of the compound had circular, walled structures for surveillance. The guards had been seen entering and leaving the enclosures, according to Rosa. "The Professor, he wrote it down. Here . . ." She pulled out a scrap of paper from a jacket pocket. "Here it is—the Professor gave me this schedule. He insisted that I keep it—for the time of the uprising. He believed that time would come. He was a great man."

Rockson looked at the scrawled schedule. The Professor, whoever the hell he had been, had been thorough. He had tracked the movements long enough to notice that it was different on even weeks than on odd weeks. This was the second week of September; that meant, according to the scrawl, that guards were relieved at 6 P.M., 2 A.M., and 10 A.M. "Two A.M.," Rock said, "We have to be as close as we can to the enclosures at Two A.M. That leaves just an hour to show you all how to conduct guerilla warfare. Long enough to learn the rudiments of garroting, and knifing a man so that he *doesn't* scream."

Barrelman, when he had finished, said, "It *will*

work. But your clothes are unsuitable! Darryl—bring the White King's garment!"

Darryl brought in a plain white karate-gi type of suit that he presented to Rockson with bowed head. "We made it for you, for when you came to release us from our bondage, as predicted by the Founder." Rockson inspected the suit. It was large enough and loose fitting, a suitable climbing garment. He quickly shucked his own clothes in a corner and donned the outfit, not for its symbolic importance to the Runners, but because the suit, being white, was good camouflage for climbing the tower. It fit perfectly, oddly enough.

"Okay," Rock ordered. "Get to your positions." He had taught them what they needed to know. Practice would come in the field. The Runners filed out of the cavern room and through the sewers to positions close to the enclosures, and one man in front of each of the four teams opened up the manhole cover enough to see out. Exactly on schedule, the guards opened up the thick doors of the enclosures and new guards approached to relieve them. Rockson was relieved to see from his vantage point that there were only three occupants to his target. With the three replacements, that made six at each corner of the compound. He hoped to hell the other teams had learned their lessons well.

"Here goes nothing," he whispered.

The guards were slow, and unprepared for the

lightning attack, for the steel slamming into their backs, for the wire necklaces that strangled the life out of them. And through the doors of the four corner enclosures that guarded the Tower compound grounds, not guards, but free men, entered.

All of this was done in a matter of a minute or two. Rockson peered through the gunslit in his compound, and saw the winking flashlight beam in the gunslits across the way. He returned the prearranged signal. Sinking down in relief next to the bulge-eyed corpse of one of the guards, he waited for the moment that the compound's intruder detectors would be momentarily cut off. *That* job was being done underground, by Darryl and his crew. The circuit breakers would be employed for a minute, no more. Hopefully, the personnel in the Tower would just think it an anomaly, if they were even looking at their readouts. Perhaps they too were as complacent as the corner guards.

Or maybe they were *waiting for him.*

Chapter 15

Rockson opened the door on the Tower side and started his run. He ducked down low and cut away from his brave band of men. He knew that many might die to cover his assault, that Bravery hides its noble face behind the most unlikely appearances. The men had acted like trained, combat-steeled Free-fighters, not like rag-clad derelicts. They had only needed a leader, a White King, to rally them to fight! Rock had instructed Barrelman to keep them hidden, ready to fire if he was detected.

As he slipped across the mall surrounding the Tower, he clung to the slightest cover. A bush, whose shadow he blended with, contained a spiderweb-fine trip-wire that would have triggered an alarm—if someone without his ninja-sense had passed that way. But no wires, no mere mechanical trap, was subtle enough to outsmart his warrior psyche. Even as he left his comrades for the solo climb that would spell the difference between success and failure on this night, he could feel himself sinking deeply into the killing-survival instinct. Every cell in his body went on emergency alert. As his inner ear and mind's eye swept the surroundings, he became aware of the slightest wind, the smallest scurrying sound of the tiniest creature. Only tuned to every moment of the fine line of life and death could he hope to survive the Chessman's sinister strategies. For this was no ordinary opponent. This was a man — if one could call the despicable mind-twisted evil, whose mental reach outstripped all others, a man. This was a man who could peer into his enemies' minds like a psychic scourge and rip out their will power. Rockson knew that he would have to be a shadow, a formless wind of death. Only then could he slip through the traps and ploys that he knew must lie between his lethal hands and the Chessman's ultimately vulnerable pale throat.

The Doomsday Warrior slipped along the shadows, taking advantage of the gentle roll of lawn to hide his muscled, bronze-hard body. He came upon a hollow in the land deep enough to afford him good cover, and close enough for him to scan the Tower and plot the details of his assault.

The ancient masters of war have always stressed that knowledge of the enemy is worth more than legions in the field. Rockson knew that he must clearly fix the *gamesman* consciousness of the Chessman in his mind before he took his step. For once the game of life and death began, the Doomsday Warrior knew, there was only will and instinct. The hands of the Doomsday Warrior were ready; they would not fail him. There was no thought that could break their grip. The futureman tuned his awareness into the rest of his body, steeling every organ, every molecule, into a carefully unified force. He must plunge deeply into the powerways that the Glowers had taught him, to make up for the lack of equipment. Only with the mind was the impossible accomplished; only with inner calm could the river of potential be unleashed.

The compound gun was in his grip. It was puny by comparison to his futureworld's weapon of choice, the Liberator rifle, but was as lethal a weapon as he could fashion with the backward technology of this time.

He snapped the beech open, pulled out the clip. Everything A-OK—a full magazine of flesh-destroying .50 caliber rounds; a smooth, well-oiled action. The gun would work for him, though to use it meant to violate the principal strategy that would keep him alive—stealth. *Ninja-stealth.* "You must enter like an invisible wind, cut down your enemies, and disappear into the night," Master Chen had taught once. "Only that way is there any hope for a lone ninja to truly succeed."

Rockson knew that if he got the Chessman and destroyed his equipment, his lackeys would then be unable to dominate and enslave the inhabitants of Salt Lake, even if he, Rockson, should die.

And with the Veil, the force field, shut off, all could flee.

His chronometer showed that the minute of power-cut was nearly over. Fifty feet to go. With all possible speed the Doomsday Warrior combat-ran to the wall of the Tower. He touched it, examined its surface with his night-keen mutant's eyes. He picked with care the fine cracks and crevices that led up to the open bell tower at the top. Too easy—an open invitation—this way would be full of traps. He moved to the south face.

He let his eyes start at the base of the Tower and move upward. A mere thirty feet off the ground they came to rest on an arched, elaborate stained-glass window. It could easily be reached, if one simply threw a rope over the horned-dragon gargoyle directly above the window and pulled himself up. Too easy — a trap. The low window was obviously going to be the most heavily protected. If he sent out an alarm by crashing through it, he knew that he would never make it to the Chessman's lair.

He circled swiftly to the east face of the Tower. It was smooth, barely a fingerhold anywhere. *This* was the way.

He searched out the first fingertip holds of the path to the Tower window high above. He'd have to trust that Chessman believed this wall unscalable. It wasn't — *quite*.

He began his ascent, steeling his mind against fear. Slowly he pulled himself, one finger and toehold after another, up the nearly sheer face of the silent Tower. The rhythm of his climb melded with the breeze that wafted above the city. He was a speck of dust, a fly; a white bird. He only looked at the minute granules of sand frozen in the surface of the concrete, the fine edge of life and death that he now held in his steely fingertips. His focused mind's KA power, its inner instinct, was at one with the process of climbing.

Climber and the Tower became one, perfect. Unable to fall.

He at last came to the overhang of the ledge just beneath the bell-tower opening. He grabbed it just as his concentration faltered. There were noises below —

people talking! He froze, looked down. The Runners weren't to expose themselves unless Rock was spotted. What had happened?

But it wasn't the Runners. He heard a pleading female voice among the heavy footfalls. A rookie squad entering the grounds of the Tower, a blond woman in their midst.

Kim. And the two children were with her.

Chapter 16

Kim! Oh, God! She wasn't really his wife, she was not the *real* Kim—and the kids weren't really his. But he couldn't let them suffer or perish at the hands of the Chessman. They hadn't done anything wrong—they couldn't be held responsible for him. They were innocent!

Rockson watched them disappear into the maw of the Tower far below him. The children were wailing, and Kim was crying and pleading with the police.

One of the policemen shouted at them as he prodded them with his stick, and his voice drifted up to Rockson.

"Quiet!" the officer bellowed. "Save it for the Chessman! Shut up and show the proper respect for the Holy Ground!"

So—Chessman himself wanted to see the "Rockman Family." The holy man would get more than he bargained for.

Rockson huddled under the ledge just below his goal, the Tower window, huddling to avoid being spotted. He clung to the sheer face like a human fly.

He saw the figures below enter the portal of the

Tower and heard the heavy door shut.

Scattered shooting and screams erupted below as the Runners were discovered by the guards and thought police. A burst of machine-gun fire peppered the Tower just above Rockson, causing him to duck even lower. Damn! Couldn't the resistance people get the upper hand? If they couldn't hold out, he would soon be outnumbered and outgunned by reinforcements. They had to hold the Tower hostage.

Rockson dodged another spray of bullets. Then, with the compound gun thrown over his shoulder as a counter-weight, he pulled himself up onto the ledge. In a quick, darting movement, he slammed the butt of his gun into the pane.

It was made of some sort of shatter-resistant material, and did not break. Cursing, he leveled the muzzle of his gun at it and let loose a short blast, hating to waste bullets on a window.

The window was not strong enough to deflect the point-blank bullets. It cracked into a web and then fell in a shower of jagged shards. Rockson knocked loose a few remaining pieces and hurled himself through the opening just as a volley of machine-gun bullets spit into the Tower around him.

He tucked and hit the floor inside on his right shoulder, rolling with the impact, holding the compound gun close to his body. In a flash he was on his feet, weapon ready to fire. But no enemy confronted him. He was alone — for the moment.

Rockson quickly sized up his surroundings. He was in a dimly-lit hallway that curved around the perimeter of the top of the Tower. Below, through the broken window, he heard sounds of fighting. Wild screams of death, the whoosh of flames.

With his back to the wall and his finger on the trigger, Rockson slid around the hallway, ready to pump lead into anything that jumped out at him. Rockson kept sliding and sliding along the smooth wall, wondering when he would hit a door or an interior window, hoping he had not struck a dead end—that the Chessman was on another level.

Then he saw it—a small, steep metal staircase that went up to the very tip of the Tower's spire. It had to lead to the Chessman's lair!

In the same instant, a black blur shot out from around the curvature of the hallway, coming head-on at Rockson. It was a guard, and he opened fire on Rockson with his submachine gun on full auto.

Rock took a chestful of lead. He cried out in pain. The impact sent him flying backward off his feet, crashing into the opposite wall. His head slammed into concrete. He saw stars and sank to the floor.

For a wild, crazy moment, he thought he was dead. The front of the white suit was ripped and burned, but there was no blood. The jacket had stopped the bullets—saved him from death. All he had suffered was a bruising from the powerful impact of the gunfire. The "White King's" clothing was bullet-resistant!

Click click. Click. The guard was firing again at Rockson, the barrel of his gun leveled at the Doomsday Warrior's head, but nothing was happening. He was out of ammunition. Cursing, he fumbled in his belt for another clip.

Rockson pushed himself up and swayed to his feet, steadying himself against the wall. He lifted his own weapon and fired in a tight arc. The guard's arms jerked, and he dropped the clip and gun. He staggered backward, screaming, but the scream was abruptly cut short when bullets tore into the man's throat. Blood burst form the severed neck like water under pressure. The guard collapsed in a heap.

Rockson wiped away the dead man's blood that had sprayed into his own eyes and went to the body. He took one remaining clip from the ammunition belt, and the emptied pistol which was still warm.

The guard wore the insignia of a knight. "Bad move," Rockson muttered as he stepped over the corpse. He leapt onto the staircase and began climbing up.

A series of rapid shots came at him from above. Bullets pinged and richocheted off the steps. Another guard was at the top of the staircase, dodging into view just long enough to squeeze off shots from his submachine gun, then ducking back out of sight.

Rockson was a vulnerable target, pinned on the stairs. Thank God, this guard was unaware of the use of ricochets, or he would be confetti by now, white suit or no.

There was nothing for him to do but go forward and up. Rockson jumped up the stairs, holding his finger down on the trigger of his gun. The noise was deafening. Bullets zinged everywhere, in careful patterns and angles.

The bullets hit home, blinding the man. As Rockson reached the top of the staircase, he quit firing and flipped the gun around to jam the stock into the midriff of the blinded man.

The man grunted as the breath was knocked from

him, and tried to push his own weapon into Rock-son's face. With a deft slice of his hand, Rockson snapped the guard's arm back; the gun clattered down the stairwell. Something else fell loose and banged down the stairs—the extra clip of bullets Rockson had taken from the dead soldier.

The guard unsheathed a knife and began jabbing wildly at Rockson. Rock twisted his face to avoid the razor-sharp blade, but not fast enough—the edge caught him on the cheek and raked a bloody trail from temple to jaw. The wound was superficial, but it hurt like hell and bled profusely.

Dropping his gun, he struggled with the guard for control of the knife. The man had incredible strength, and Rockson's muscles strained to keep the knife-point out of his throat. Blood was running from the man's shattered eyes.

He grasped the guard's wrist and twisted his hand around until the blade was pointing in toward the man's body. He made a hard thrust. The twisting knife pierced the man's side, and he screamed. Rockson hit him in the throat with his fist, causing the guard to lose consciousness. He slumped to the floor. He would be out for at least an hour.

The guard had been the last line of exterior defense for a single, unmarked door. The Chessman's door, Rockson surmised. There was no knob; the door opened by handprint. The print-reader was imbedded in the wall to the right.

Rockson's chest was heaving as he tried to catch his breath. The wound on his face was still bleeding, the warm blood trickling down his throat. He wiped at it with the back of his hand.

209

In a sudden lull in the noise around the Tower, Rockson heard voices from within the Chessman's chamber. A woman's voice — Kim's! The guards must have taken her and the children inside through some other stairwell. A man's voice — no doubt the Chessman's — was speaking to her in an angry tone, but the words were indistinguishable. He had to get in!

There was only one way to get the knobless door open. Rockson raised his compound gun and fired.

The door was made out of a super-strong alloy that could deflect most machine-gun fire, but the compound gun was no ordinary weapon. The bullets tore into the door. Rockson concentrated his fire along the right side of the jamb where the locking mechanism should be mounted. He fired until the metal was blasted and smoking.

The gunfire broke the door's seal. Rockson finished the job by kicking and shoving until he had an opening big enough for him to squeeze through.

He stepped inside, the hot, smoking machine gun in his hands.

"Teddy!" screamed Kim. She was backed against the right wall, cowering, clutching her two children to her. Her face was streaked with tears, her hair wild and disheveled.

But Rockson only took fleeting notice of her. Directly in front of him stood a tall, thin man in a blinding red outfit that flashed like a starfield. It hurt Rock's eyes. His face was concealed in a white mask from forehead to chin. A shock of silver-gray hair flowed above the mask.

The Chessman.

Far below, on the grounds of Temple Square, Barrelman and his army of revolutionaries desperately battled the well-armed rookies and Tower guards. The area around the square was in chaos, filled with gunfire, smoke, artillery blasts, screams, and shouting. Barrelman hoped they could hold out long enough.

Their years of stealth and practiced "invisibility" had worked to the Runners' advantage in the early stages of the assault. As Rockson had begun his ascent, they had slipped around the Tower and managed to take out nearly all of the laser searchbeams. Other floodlights still bathed the grounds, but they could not be used to zero in on a lone figure scaling the wall.

As Rockson had neared the top of the spire, the Runners had launched their attack, diverting the ground police.

For many of the Runners, it was a suicidal offensive. Barrelman and the rest had known it would be, and had accepted it. A few deaths would be a small price if Salt Lake City could be liberated from the Chessman. "Live free or die," was the chant.

The Runners had quickly picked off the sentries around the perimeter of the square. Now guards had mobilized at parapets along the brick wall that enclosed the grounds, firing at the Runners with machine guns and hand-held rocket launchers.

The Runners dug in to their hiding places, firing back and hurling grenades. The grenades had to be used sparingly; they didn't have many.

The man next to Barrelman was hit by machine-gun fire and slumped over his weapon. He was dead. His name was Fortier, and he was a young fellow, a recent recruit to the Runners. Barrelman felt a moment of sadness, then sighted his machine gun and fired up at the figures moving along the parapet. He heard a scream, and hoped it was because of one of his bullets.

He looked up at the Tower, white and cold in the light from the Temple grounds. "You've got to get him, Rock," he said out loud, for only himself to hear. "You've got to!"

Rockson was fixated by the Chessman. He looked like a living skeleton — a skull with hair and a mask, gaunt limbs barely more than the bones themselves. He couldn't be human! Rockson thought.

"Rockman . . ." the Chessman said, his voice sounding like it came from a tomb. "Rockman, you have sinned . . ."

"The only sin I've committed is the desire to be free!" Rockson shouted back. He tightened his grip on his gun.

The Chessman's icy blue eyes, intense and full of hate pierced through him. The eyes radiated an incredible, powerful energy force, drawing him under a spell. The red of the Chessman's garment was so bright it nearly blinded him. Rockson put up a hand as though he were shielding his eyes from brilliant sunlight.

The Chessman's thin pale lips moved. "Lay down your weapon, Theodore Rockman, and come *here*." He raised a bony arm and pointed a finger at

Rockson. The nails on the bleached hands were dark blue.

The urge to obey the deep voice and the piercing eyes was overwhelming. With great effort, Rockson tore his eyes away. He glanced at Kim and the children, still whimpering and cowering in a corner. "Get back, Kim," he said. "As far as possible."

Kim responded by pulling the children closer to her and backing away. But in a round room, there were no corners to hide in.

The door . . . Rockson must bar the door before more thought police arrived.

Rockson took a step toward the door. His feet moved like blocks of lead. The Chessman was commanding him to come hither, and the resistance took every ounce of his will. His hands too were like lead; he couldn't raise the submachine gun.

"Don't disobey!" cried Kim. "Give yourself up, Teddy! The Chessman has promised mercy if you do!"

Rockson ignored her. *Help me, brothers*, he called out silently to the Glowers. *Power . . . Focus . . .*

Rockson summoned his inner power, calling on it to protect him from the magnetic, hypnotic influence of the Chessman. He seemed to be moving in slow motion. He reached the door . . . pushed it shut . . . then, clasping his gun to his chest with his left hand and shoving with his right, he barricaded the door with a heavy metal cabinet.

Rockson felt the Chessman's eyes boring into the back of his head. He turned to face the skeletal being again. The Chessman had moved forward, almost gliding rather than walking. The dreadful aspect of a spectre, not a man.

Kim and the children shrank further back. "Teddy," Kim pleaded. "Don't! For the sake of our *children*, Teddy . . ."

"Be quiet!" Rockson shut out her words. He had to focus, concentrate on his own inner source of *power*.

He silently repeated the chants that would put him in an altered state of consciousness, all the while keeping his conscious mind alert. "Om ga-te, ga-te, para-san-ga-te . . ."

"Stop right there," he commanded the Chessman, who was looming over him. God, the man was tall! The very air around him crackled with static electricity. The garment was dazzling, filling Rockson's vision. If he came any closer, Rockson felt, he would smother in the all-encompassing redness. Rockson pointed the compound gun at the leering skull. "You're finished, Chessman. No more king of the board! No more master of the game! No more slaves!" He pressed his finger against the trigger.

The gun spit air. The ammunition clip was empty. Rockson had emptied all his remaining bullets into the door.

The eyes behind the white mask bored harder into Rockson. The dry lips moved. "You're the one who's finished, Rockman. There will be no reprieve from this act of disobedience. I am greater than you!"

Rockson thrust the butt end at the Chessman's face, but the holy man's skeletal fingers closed around the barrel and ripped it from his grasp as easily as an adult would grab a baby's toy. He hurled the submachine gun away with such force that the barrel bent as it smashed into the wall.

Rockson stared at his empty hands in astonishment. The Chessman closed in, his icy breath on Rockson's face. The blue eyes were whirlpools growing larger and larger.

Rockson pushed against the gaunt form. It was hard, like steel. The Chessman's psychic force was dissolving his ability to resist. He fought back with all his mental strength. But suddenly Rockson's inner defense broke. He was swept away in a tidal wave of psychic energy and confusing visions. Physically, he felt the Chessman seize him in a painful, pincerlike grasp. But what he saw was not the Chessman, but a giant sea crustacean, twenty feet tall. Huge black globes of eyes waved at him on long stalks, and antennae bounced up and down. The pincers threatened to cut him in half. The creature screeched in fury.

Rockson was nearly paralyzed with fear. The Chessman, Kim and the children had vanished, replaced by this writhing monster. It was real! He felt the shell, the sensor-hairs that covered the edges of the pincers. What had happened?

Barrelman's words came back to him: *"He has a face like a skull, and powers beyond belief. Powers of Illusion . . ."*

The creature dragged him up through the air toward its mandible mouth, which was ringed with tiny, needle-sharp teeth. Rockson struggled but could not free himself of the pincer. The shell was impervious to his fists. He pulled a long-bladed knife from his pants waist and plunged it at the shell. The knife-point bounced back, barely making a dent.

The mandible worked furiously in anticipation.

215

The cavity was huge. The creature tilted Rockson, pointing him headfirst toward its mouth.

Rockson lashed out with his knife, severing one of the bobbing black eye-globes. It splatted on the floor. The crustacean shrieked and dropped Rockson.

He took the impact on his side, rolling to absorb the shock. The creature, consumed in pain, was thrashing about, waving its gigantic pincers.

Rockson got to his feet, dodging the multiple legs. He ran to the tail and climbed up on the slippery shell-back, clawing his way forward to the head.

The creature tried vainly to throw him off. Rockson held firm, and when he reached the crest of the head, just in back of the eye-stalks, he stabbed his knife deep between two sections of shell, destroying the creature's nerve center. The monster died in a wild seizure of throes.

Suddenly it vanished. The creature hadn't been real at all, but a hideous hallucination. The room returned to the way it had been, with Rockson facing the Chessman, and Kim and the children whimpering in the background.

The Chessman leered at him. Before the stunned Rockson could react, the bony form vanished again.

In the same instant, Rockson was no longer on his feet, but was being bounced on a solid, moving sheet of insect backs. The room was filled with giant cockroaches, some three to four feet long, teeming and crawling over each other. Their stench was unbearable. They were glittery and iridescent, like the radioactive, mutant cockroaches from Rockson's world. And they were more than that — somehow he knew they were meat-eaters.

Rockson struggled to stay on top. If he went under those churning, hairy legs, they would have his bones stripped in seconds. He couldn't believe it was another hallucination—it was too *real*. He could *feel* their greasy shells. They were just like the ones he had seen a few miles away from Century City once . . .

Century City! The thought went through Rockson like a bolt of lighting. The Chessman was pulling images from his own mind to create hallucinations! They seemed so real because, to Rockson, the memories *were* real. Rockson was being forced to meet his own enemies.

The Doomsday Warrior renewed his effort to focus his inner power. The KA force was still there, weakened, but pulsating. He concentrated, chanting the mantras the Glowers had taught him. The cockroaches were creations in his own mind; he could vanquish them. *"All the Power that Is and Ever Was flows through me now,"* he whispered to himself. *"The Power is here for me to command. I command the Power to lock away past thoughts and memories."*

As abruptly as they had appeared, the cockroaches evaporated, and Rockson found himself lying on his back in the Chessman's chamber, looking up at the thin red form standing over him. He sprang to his feet. "I'm on to your mind trick, Chessman," he said. "It won't work anymore." He lunged up at the pale, gaunt throat.

The Chessman blocked him, the strength in his bony claws equal to Rockson's battle-toughened muscles. The Chessman's eyes still pierced him, like sunlight intensified by a magnifying glass that catches paper on fire. The Chessman could no longer make

Rock hallucinate, but he still possessed awesome hypnotic powers.

They strained against each other, neither getting the advantage for more than a few seconds. Rockson put all his strength into pushing the Chessman back toward a window at the curved rear of the chamber.

To his right, Kim had sprung into action herself. Seeing that her "husband" was determined to destroy the Chessman—an evil act he could not possibly succeed in, and which mean certain torture and death for her and the children—she was trying her best to thwart him. If the Chessman realized she didn't support her husband, perhaps he would grant her and the children clemency.

Kim fell on Rockson's back, beating him with her tiny fists. He shrugged her off and she came at him again, pounding harder, yelling, her fragile voice lost in the sounds of the scuffle. She lost her grip as the two men crashed to the floor and rolled, bodies locked together.

She got unsteadily to her feet and looked frantically for a heavy object, intending to bash Rockson on the head. Then, over the racket, she heard pounding and shouts.

Someone was on the other side of the door! Guards!

Kim scrambled to the barricaded door. "Help!" she cried. "Help! He's trying to kill the Chessman!"

In response came a furious pounding. "Open the door!" a gruff voice shouted.

Kim got as close to the door as she could. "I can't—it's blocked, and I can't move it." She pushed on the cabinet, but her little body was no match for its heft and bulk. The kids ran to help her move it.

The pounding continued, then sounds of several men trying to push the door open took its place. The barricade held.

Rockson had the Chessman nearly to the window. He pulled back his fist and delivered a rapid series of blows to the emaciated body. A lesser man would have been crippled, but the Chessman barely flinched. He grabbed Rockson by the throat, his sharp blue nails digging into the flesh.

Rockson gasped. *To the window . . . to the window . . .* If he could just get the Chessman to lose his balance and fall through the stained-glass window.

His windpipe was completely choked off. He clawed at the hands around his throat. He couldn't get air. Seconds went by. The Chessman squeezed harder. Rockson's chest ached, his heart hammered against his ribs. He had about a minute, at best, to live.

Chapter 17

The Chessman's hands felt like a vise around Rockson's throat. Rockson gagged and choked. The edges of his vision started to go black, fuzzy. He felt dizzy, spinning off into space.

He had succeeded in pushing the Chessman back to the wall, near the window, but he didn't have the strength to go on. His lungs were on the verge of bursting for lack of air.

There was a thunderous crash, and pieces of glass and debris imploded into the chamber. The Chessman howled and arched his back; Kim and the children screamed. Rockson summoned up his last reserve of strength and pulled free of the Chessman's grasp, pushing the man away from him at the same time. The sharp blue nails raked across his throat as he spun away, gasping and wheezing for precious air.

Someone on the grounds below evidently had fired some sort of projectile into the window. The Chessman, closest to the window and with his back to it, had caught some of the shrapnel, and was groaning in pain. His garment was full of small holes.

The two were saved from more serious injury—and death—because they had been slightly to one side of the window. The Chessman's hypnotic spell had been broken. For now.

An amplified voice came from the compound below. "This is Barrelman, Chessman. If you are still alive, know that it won't be for long. Produce our leader at the window or die."

So that's what happened, Rock realized. They believe me captured or dead!

Despite his pain, the Chessman still possessed his hypnotic power. He grabbed Rockson and thrust him toward the window. "Tell them you are here—then we finish our contest!"

But the holy man's spell on the Doomsday Warrior was permanently broken, and Rockson lunged at him.

A pair of RPGs came from the ground below, and missed the Tower window, expending themselves on the impregnable stone walls. Barrelman's army was sure he was dead, and were using rocket launchers— trying to avenge him. Soon they would hit both the Doomsday Warrior and his opponent. Not to mention Kim and the kids, who were flat-out on the floor, trying to avoid being hit.

Rockson saw the control panel now; it was marked *Force field, City-encircling*. There were a set of switches. The Veil projector. He tried to reach it, but Chessman's clawing hands bent him slowly in the opposite direction. There would be another RPG soon, then another, until they were all killed. He had to end this!

With Chen's "number-five twist," Rockson slammed the Chessman backward into the window opening. The Chessman teetered and fell, but not far. He landed on the ledge that ringed the top of the

Tower. Rockson scrambled out and threw himself on top of him. The Runners on the ground stopped firing, cheered.

Rockson had the upper hand now. The Chessman was wounded, and his hypnotism no longer worked on the Doomsday Warrior. But the man had an amazing reservoir of physical strength, and it was all Rockson could do to keep from being hurled over the side of the parapet to his death.

He stabbed his fingers in the Chessman's throat. The Chessman gagged and jabbed at Rockson's eyes, missing them by millimeters. The Chessman's breaths were coming hard; he was tiring!

The Chessman bit and clawed his way out of Rockson's grasp, then dove for the window opening. Rockson tackled him as he was halfway in, dragging him back to the parapet. The Chessman twisted and fought like a rabid beast.

Rockson struggled to his feet, shoved the Chessman against the ledge. He ripped off the white mask—and gasped. It was Streltsy, his gold tooth gleaming with his words. "You shouldn't be surprised. You are not the only one with a counterpart in this world! We find ourselves matched again. Only I am much more powerful in this place than I was in the desert. I, fittingly, replaced a giant—the Chessman. You are a mere mortal. Aren't you afraid? I beat you before, after all. And future-history repeats itself. Now."

"Streltsy! Your world is about to be vaporized by an atomic attack. Don't you know this is September eleventh, 1989? Don't you realize what's about to happen?"

Chessman rushed around the corner of the tower.

He peered around the corner at Rockson. "Shall we play ring-around-the-rosy? I can run faster than you, come up behind you."

"Streltsy, you're a fool, not powerful at all. I suppose you expect your force field—the Veil—to protect your city, so that you can keep living here, keep terrorizing the city."

"Yes! I *like* it here, Rockson. I had little possibility in our other world of running anything except that damned outpost. Here, I have it all."

"You must listen. The Veil isn't powerful enough to stop a nuke explosion—a damned car can almost penetrate it! I know, I've tried. You're not keeping the city safe; you're dooming yourself and everyone in the city to death. Shut off the Veil, let everyone flee the city."

Chessman's head *disappeared*. And before Rock could turn, the Chessman was upon him, from behind, strangling, using the powers of his mind to weaken Rockson's resistance. Instead of the Chessman, Rock felt the coiling strength of a giant anaconda about his neck.

It was so unexpected, so shocking, that Rockson nearly let himself fall. His enemy seized the moment to strike out with his fists, but Rockson recovered in a violent surge of fury. "Streltsy—you will *die* for what you did to me!"

Rockson twisted into a flurry of bony fists and landed a solid punch of his own, square in the Chessman's solar plexus. The gaunt man reeled backward as the breath was knocked from him. Rockson launched a roundhouse kick to the head. Streltsy lost his balance, teetering for a breathless moment. Then he plunged over the side, screaming.

The scream ended swiftly in a sudden sickening thud. Rockson, oblivious to bullets, looked down just in time to see the Chessman bounce on the horn of the dragon gargoyle above the low window. The mangled body—nearly torn in half by the horn—hit the side of the Tower and continued its plunge to the ground. It hit the walkway with a sickening splat, like that of a melon bursting open, bouncing once and then rolling to rest. The shooting stopped.

A mighty cheer rose up from below. Rockson saw some of the Runners coming out of their cover, waving and shouting with joy. They hugged each other, unmindful that they were exposing themselves to enemy guns.

"Don't stop!" he shouted, knowing his words wouldn't carry. "It's not over yet!" Even as he shouted, the rookies below were taking aim on the Runners who had dropped their guard.

He groaned as he watched several of them take bullets and go down. The other Runners who jumped out into the open scattered back to cover and resumed firing. In the midst of the turmoil, Rockson saw one of the city's brush-eaters come slowly down the boulevard, hugging the curb, its scoop in the front pulling debris into the metal mouth. Even on this killing field, someone was busily cleaning Salt Lake City's streets, oblivious to the madness around.

None of the battling fighters paid any attention to the machine, either, as it churned down the street toward the Tower grounds, its headlight beams searching for things to pick up. Rockson saw that the Chessman's remains were directly in the brush-eater's path.

Eddie had heard the shooting, and the crackling radio in his twenty-five-ton man-eating machine had told the story—the damned homeless derelicts were storming City Hall Tower!

He had swung his machine around, heading the huge brush-eater out of the park and toward the action. Nobody was going to hurt the Chessman.

It took a full ten minutes to get to the square, and as he tore through the gate, gears grinding wildly, eating up fences, shrubbery—anything that stood in his way—he laughed madly. The windows of his night-prowling hellish death-dealer cracked and shattered as bullets hit at odd angles. Pieces of glass flew about and stuck in his cap, his shoulders. Blood trickled down his hand holding the ten-gear shift. But onward he plunged. Give me a target, he thought, looking at the screen—someone that doesn't move too fast . . .

Suddenly the radar showed a blip. The autofocus high-intensity headlights zeroed in on a fallen figure on the pavement—a tall thin man wearing a torn robe. Not a rookie or knight, nor blue-blazered consultant . . . therefore—an enemy!

Laughing like a maniac, Eddie turned the brush-eater and roared at the fallen man.

From high above, Rockson watched as the machine drew closer, eating up debris, until it reached the Chessman and stopped. The body was twitching. The

225

scooper tried to suck it in. For an awful minute, the scoop sucked away at the Chessman, the engine whining with the effort. Then the pitch of the motor went up as the eager driver tried to adjust to its obstacle. The tearing teeth came out, and with a buzzsaw-like noise they consumed what was left of the evil dictator.

With a cough, the machine deposited the body parts inside and then continued on its way, leaving only a bloody stain behind on the pavement.

Rockson pulled away from the parapet. He had one more job to do. The Chessman might be dead, but his spell on the city wasn't yet broken. He had to turn off the Veil machine.

He crawled back through the shattered window into the chamber. The children were huddled on the floor, and Kim was still struggling to free the door of its barricade.

"Kim, it's almost over," he said gently, pulling her away from the door, avoiding her tiny fists that flailed in his face. "The Chessman is dead."

Stunned, she stopped struggling. "Dead?" She could hardly believe it. "The Chessman is dead?" She stumbled away from him in a daze. "No!"

Rockson looked around the chamber. There. There was the control panel. He leapt to it, ready to flick the switches at random. But he noticed a reminder Chessman had made to himself. A small scrawl at the lower switch. *"Remember, turn the Veil off only in coded sequence."* Rockson hesitated. The code had been lost with the Chessman's death. What would happen if he didn't pull them in sequence? An explosion? Think!

But there wasn't time to think. He'd have to chance it; the Veil had to come down. He pulled the switches from right to left. Nothing happened. No explosion. Then a readout came across the small screen on the console: UNAUTHORIZED SHUTDOWN SEQUENCE, VEIL SEALED IN "ON" POSITION, AS PROGRAMMED.

Rockson had made a mistake. He'd sealed the city like a tomb! The only way out now would be through the Portal. *Maybe.*

And to convince the citizens to follow him to the portal, he'd at least have to shut off the mind-control muzik.

Though the muzik was broadcast from the radio tower at the Tabernacle, the Chessman must have controlled it from here. Where was the control? Rockson called upon his inner psychic energy, commanding mind-force to let him match the thoughtprint of a dead man. It could be done if he tried hard enough. It *had* to be done.

Muzik control, he thought steadily, focusing his power. He imaged himself as the Chessman, seeing himself in his mind as he reached out to flick a switch, turn a knob, press a button—whatever would click. He felt a dark, unpleasant energy fill his mind—the Black Force that controlled the Chessman and gave him his power—and he fought to keep it from obliterating his senses.

Muzik control . . . muzik control . . .

Suddenly Rockson realized he was staring at it—a long, narrow panel that had appeared to be merely ornamental. This time there was only one switch. On-off. Rockson flicked it to the off position. Success.

The air went silent, except for sounds of scattered

gunfire, and that, too, went quickly silent. For the first time in God-knew-how-many-years, Salt Lake City was completely quiet.

In the blink of an eye, night became day. The sun rose in a sky that went from black to pearly rose to bright blue; the city sparkled and gleamed and, for a brief moment, bustled with its usual activity.

Then a hush fell as people realized the hypno-music had stopped. At first, many of the citizens didn't know exactly what had happened—only that something was wrong, dreadfully wrong. All but the oldest residents had been programmed their entire lives by thought control, and without a voice whispering to their brains, telling them what to do and how to behave and how to think, they were suddenly disoriented. And the longer the air was silent, the more disoriented they became.

In the glittering glass-and-concrete skyscrapers, workers stopped at their tasks and stared questioningly at one another. It was a glitch, they thought—somewhere a circuit had broken. The Chessman would get it fixed, the muzik would resume, and life would go on as normal.

In the streets, pedestrians halted in midstride, and then looked around them as though they found themselves in an alien place. Buses, cars, and trucks sat unmoving on the wide boulevards, despite the changing of the traffic lights.

In restaurants, diners put down their silverware and stared stupidly at the food on their plates, as if it no longer tasted good or they had bitten into something bitter. In shops and stores, half-naked zombies wandered out of dressing rooms, and no one stopped them from stepping out onto the streets.

Within minutes after the muzik halted, the broadcast airwaves went dead. The television programmers and radio announcers sat frozen in their chairs, not knowing which buttons to push or what to say. They had never thought for themselves. At the Holy Network, the city's only television station, someone had the presence of mind to flip a switch and go off the air; snow and static replaced the image of Bishop Pohsib, who had turned into a stuttering dummy.

For what seemed like an eternity, Salt Lake City and every living creature in it was petrified, waiting for the muzik to resume.

But the muzik did not resume, and so anxious chattering and murmuring began to fill the silence: "What's going on?" "What happened?" "What are we doing?" "What are we *supposed* to do?" The Chessman had never issued instructions to anyone—even his lieutenants—for actions to take if the hypno-music ceased because as far as the Chessman was concerned, the muzik never would stop.

Uncertainty began giving way to fear and panic. Though the hypno-music was a powerful control, no one was completely normal yet, because of the tranquilized food and water. Paranoia gripped thousands, who started to run blindly through the streets as though being chased by unseen monsters. Others crawled under desks and chairs or hid in closets, crying and whimpering like children.

Those who were naturally aggressive—but whose tendencies had been damped by drugs—became antagonistic. Diners dumped their food on the floor and threw it at the walls. Some even marched into the kitchens and threw the food at the cooks, shouting about bad taste and poor quality: "Hell, we ain't gonna pay for *this* crap!" People who had never uttered obscenities — a crime in the Chessman's state — were swearing blue streaks, reveling in temper tantrums they had always secretly wanted to have.

Some people reacted with fits of glee and hysteria, cackling and shrieking and doing cartwheels. They jumped out of their cars and hung out of building windows, waving and shouting incoherently at no one in particular. They turned on fire hydrants and danced like maniacs in the sprays.

Others — distinctly in the minority — strove valiantly to maintain control and resume their normal activities. Most of these people were dazed, however, and acted more like whacky automatons who didn't realize what they were doing. Gas-station attendants filled cars through the radiators instead of gas tanks; garbage collectors dumped out the contents of cans all over yards.

At the City Detention and Rehabilitation Center, the guards let out all the prisoners — who promptly rounded up the obliging guards and put *them* in the cells.

Chaos reigned throughout the city. The thought police — those who still had presence of mind due to a more-thorough programming than that given the average citizen — were powerless to stem the tide. Any officer who tried to discipline a citizen with his stick was jumped by dozens of vengeful men and women. Most of the police made a cursory effort to restore order and then fled for their lives. Duty went only so far!

At the Tabernacle the scene was no different. Guards dropped their weapons and roamed aimlessly, babbling a stream of nonsense syllables. Some rushed up to Runners, hugging and kissing them like long-lost brothers. Others just went crazy and staggered about with their hands in the air shouting, "I surrender! I surrender!"

Of all the people in the city, the only ones who did have control were the Runners, whose systems were free of drugs. A euphoric Barrelman shouted at his subordinates to seize the Tower itself. "Round up the guards — get their weapons! The city is ours! Winston — take the radio center and broadcast a message to the people! Tell them we're all free! Tell them they can do *anything they want*!"

Rockson went back out to the parapet at the top of the Tower and watched the disintegration of the Chessman's regime, worried about what he was witnessing. The chaos and the abrupt change from night to day signaled a disruption in the time warp. Rockson seemed to be the only one aware of the time slip — everyone else, Runners included, preoccupied with the headiness of freedom.

Looking out across the city, Rockson could barely make out the clock on the city-government tower. Good God! The hands were moving — way too fast.

The city was out of the time warp, advancing to zero hour — the moment when nuclear bombs would devastate it, and kill the inhabitants.

Rockson was horrified. He had wanted only to free himself from the prison of the time warp, so that he

231

could get back to his own continuum, and free the people from the living death of an oppressive dictator. But he had failed. Sure, they were free of the muzik, but they were entombed.

"The nukes will come!" he cried out to himself. "I can't change history! Salt Lake City will be destroyed. It was bombed to ruins!"

There was no time to debate probables and possibles. One thing was certain: If Rockson couldn't get through the Portal before the bombs hit — if he couldn't get out of the time warp and back into the future — then he would perish along with everyone else. He could vanish into nothingness, a human being who never existed, the Doomsday Warrior who never was.

But he had to save more than himself. He owed survival to a few — the wife and children of his parallel personality, Theodore Rockman, and to Barrelman and the brave Runners, without whose help he would not have succeeded. He had to tell them what was happening — had to save them! Somehow.

Poor creatures, he thought with sadness, their freedom will be short-lived.

Could he convince them they were on the brink of a nuclear war? These oppressed souls who probably knew nothing of the outside world? Would any of them *listen* to him in their euphoria. Was stopping the muzik enough?

In the distance, the clock hands were moving faster.

Chapter 18

Rockson looked for the source of the sobbing. Kim was sitting on the floor trying to comfort her crying children, Teddy junior and Barbara.

"Kim, take the children! We've got to get out of here!"

Kim shrank away from him. "Don't touch me, you monster! You're not the Teddy I loved and married! I don't know who you are! You've destroyed *everything*!"

"Kim, you don't understand—"

"I do understand! You went crazy and killed the Chessman. You've ruined our lives! Now what are we going to do?" Her anger dissolved into a torrent of tears. The children mimicked her and renewed their crying.

Rockson threw his hands up in the air. "For God's sakes, pull yourself together! I haven't got time to explain everything, but believe me, we must leave the city as fast as we can!"

Kim sniffled. "Of course you want to get out. The police will be after you. You want to take us hostage!"

"The police aren't going after anyone. They're laying down their weapons. Don't you see? Everyone is free—there is no more mind programming. You can do as you please—whatever you want."

"Do as I please?" said Kim, bewildered. "You mean I have to decide for myself what to do?"

"Not exactly," said Rockson, exasperated. They were wasting precious time! "*I'll* tell you what to do. Follow my instructions."

"Oh, no, Teddy—you're crazy. I don't trust you anymore." Fresh tears poured down her cheeks as she put her head in her hands.

Rockson bent down to comfort her, and gently pulled her to her feet. "Don't do it for yourself—do it for the children. You want them to be all right, don't you?"

Kim nodded.

"Then, take them and come with me. No one will harm them, or you."

"But where will we go?"

"Away from the city."

Teddy junior scrambled to his feet and looked defiantly up at Rockson. "Forget it, *Daddy-o*. You're not making us go anywhere! I'm with Mom!" He glared up at Rock with his little fists clenched.

Rockson was astonished at the defiance of this pint-sized boy. Was this the same Teddy junior who had obediently followed every command, who had sat quietly through dinner and gone to bed early without complaint?

Barbara joined in with her older brother, scowling up at him with her lower lip stuck out in a nasty pout. "We're gonna turn you over to the cops for being bad," she hollered.

Rockson wanted to turn both of them over his knee

234

and give them a good spanking. Free will *did* have its drawbacks.

If he had been in his own time continuum and these were free children, he would not have hesitated to give them a sound thrashing. But how did one discipline children who were supposed to be your own — who called you "Dad"? Rockson, every brawny inch of him, felt helpless in the face of this juvenile rebelliousness.

He was also angry that time was slipping by while his "family" squabbled. He screwed up his face and bellowed, "Do as I say if you know what's good for you!"

Kim and the children blanched. Theodore Rockman, mild-mannered C.P.A., had never sounded so mean, so potentially *violent*.

"Yes, dear," Kim said in a meek voice. "Children, you heard your father."

"That's better," grumbled Rockson, stalking to the barricaded door. He pushed aside the metal cabinet with one quick heave, his show of strength clearly impressing Kim and the kids. The rebellion was quickly forgotten.

"Wow!" said Teddy junior. "I wanna be like that when I grow up!"

If he grows up, thought Rockson grimly. He kicked and battered open the door and motioned impatiently for them to step on it and get out.

Outside the chamber, the guards who had been trying to break in were standing around chatting and smoking as though nothing were wrong. "Hello, Mr. Rockman!" one of them boomed, taking off his helmet and making a sweeping bow. "And Mrs.

235

Rockman and the little ones! Is there anything we can do for you?" Evidently these guards had lost their aggressiveness.

"Yes," Rock said. "Get us safely out of the grounds and to a car."

"Right this way," the guard said, heading off down the hallway. "There should be plenty of cars parked around the square. You can have your pick!" He led them to an elevator, discovered it no longer worked, then ushered them to a stairwell. "It's a long way down — I'll carry the little one," he offered.

The guard took Barbara while Rockson handled Teddy junior. They clumped down the spiral staircase. At ground level, legs aching, the men put the children down and the guard led them out of the compound, taking the shortest path.

Outside the walls, Rockson searched for Barrelman. He had to warn the Runners, talk them into leaving their victory and getting out of town.

But finding Barrelman or any of the Runners wasn't going to be easy. Salt Lake City was burning.

The fear, panic, and disorientation of the freed citizens had erupted into full-scale pandemonium in sections of the city — particularly in the chessboard blocks that fanned out from the Tower Square. The controls were off, and no one knew how to restore order. The people were like children set free from over-controlling parents to run amok.

Throngs of wild-eyed looters were smashing into store windows, grabbing anything they could get their hands on. They reveled in the sheer joy of being berserk, not wanting what they stole, just taking things and hurling them onto the pavement. Self-appointed fire-starters with homemade torches dashed about the streets, igniting anything flammable that caught their eyes. Flames exploded windows and roared skyward. Fire was everywhere.

Rockson watched briefly as three thought police, desperately trying to stop looters, were backed into a wall by an angry mob that pounced on them and began beating them to death. Nearby, a lone rookie saw what was happening—and saw there was no escape from more angry people who were closing in. He put his gun to his head and fired.

Rockson grimaced and shielded the children as best as he could. The scenes around them were awful, but he was powerless to do anything about them.

Beside him, Kim reacted like a horse in a burning barn, not wanting to move; the children were growing wide-eyed with fear. He pulled on her arm. "Come on!" He herded the three of them across the boulevard and into the park, where he tucked them into the bushes that the Runners had used for cover as they sneaked around the Temple Square. "Stay here—don't move," he commanded. "I'll be back in a few minutes."

"But where are you going?" shrieked Kim.

"I've got to find someone—a friend."

"Don't leave us!"

"I'll be back!" Rockson took off at a lope, searching for Barrelman. The stocky revolutionary wouldn't have left the area, he reasoned; he'd be too busy making sure the Chessman's headquarters were all entirely neutralized. Rockson stopped several Runners and asked if they'd seen their leader. He also instructed them to go to the spot where he'd left Kim and the children. He had something important to disclose, he said.

At last Rockson found Barrelman, who was rounding up a group of docile guards who were to be held prisoner in the Tower until order was established.

"Rock!" he shouted when he sighted the Doomsday Warrior. "The fires — we've got to stop the burning! But there's no one to man the fire trucks — they've all gone berserk!"

"Forget it. And leave them, too." Rockson jerked a thumb at the guards, who were staring at him and Barrelman with moronic grins.

"What! I can't leave them. What if one of them picks up a gun—"

"There's no time to explain. Just *do* it. Get as many Runners as possible together and come with me." Rockson was already pushing on the short, squat body, forcing Barrelman to go along with him. He took quick, long strides, and the little man stumbled to keep up with him.

"But, Rock—"

"Shut up." Rockson's tone was friendly but firm. "Once I had to trust you without explanation. Now you've got to do the same."

Barrelman looked bewildered. "Okay, Rock." He whistled at two Runners up ahead, motioning them to come along.

The chaos in the city continued unabated as Rockson gathered his small group near the park benches. The noise was punctuated by sounds of gunfire. Either ammunition was exploding in the flames or

238

some of the wilder citizens were going on shooting sprees. Bullets whined through the air.

Rockson led his group to the safety of a building across the park that proved open but deserted. He pushed them all inside the door, shut it, and turned to face the group. "I've got something to tell you," he began, speaking swiftly. "It's hard to believe, but you must trust that I know the truth. You all know that I am not really one of you, that I am from another place—and time.

"The Veil that surrounds Salt Lake City is not a natural barrier, though that's what you all think." The faces around Rockson looked skeptical, but he went on. "For some reason, Salt Lake City got stuck in time—it's hard to explain. I really can't. But today is the day of World War Three. Today is Doomsday. A nuclear war will destroy not only this city, but nearly all the cities of the world. I hope we can escape back to where I come from—the world one hundred years after the bomb-blasts."

A gasp rose up from his audience. Outside, the noise escalated, and Rockson had to raise his voice. "The death of the Chessman and the end of the muzik has jolted the city out of the time warp. The clock is moving forward, quickly, to zero hour. I've been in the Portal several times, and was transported through space, but not time. I believe it will become a *time portal* at the instant of zero hour. I hope I'm right. If so, some of us might be saved, if we go through."

Barrelman grabbed his sleeve, gazing up into his face. "Rock! How can this be? Is this really true?"

"I don't understand the whys myself—I just know what's going to happen. You've got to believe me if you want to live!" There was no sense mentioning it might not work.

"But how can we survive nuclear missiles?"

"By getting out of the city and going through the Portal, like I said. Don't try to understand, just do it."

"When is zero hour? How much time do we have?"

"If I remember my history correctly, the missiles will strike at four minutes after six tonight. Time itself is altering; I don't know how much time we have left to escape—the clocks are moving erratically, but faster and faster."

"This is preposterous!" someone shouted. "I don't believe it!" Others joined in the chorus of disbelief.

Rockson shrugged. "That is your decision. I can't elaborate—you'll have to take it on faith, those of you who want to believe. I'm leaving, and I'm taking Kim and the kids with me. I hope the rest of you will follow. Get a car, a truck—any vehicle you can find—and head for the dump at the outskirts of town, where the Portal is. Don't stop to gather possessions, but take as many friends as you can."

With that, Rockson drew his family toward him and turned to leave. He stopped at Barrelman and stuck out his hand, looking the short man directly in the eye. "Brother," he said, "thank you. I know you're a survivor. Now save yourself."

Barrelman immediately began mobilizing his people, shouting at them to commandeer vehicles and round up as many Runners as could be found.

Rockson spotted an abandoned taxicab a couple of blocks away. He scooped up both children, and he and Kim ran for it. His Seiko said 5:30—and he could

240

see the minute hand moving!

He shoved the kids in the back seat, and Kim scrambled in beside him onto the front seat. The keys were still in the ignition. The cab, like the Porsche, was similar to vehicles in his world, and Rockson had no trouble revving up the engine and slamming it into gear. The cab screeched off, burning rubber for the entire length of a block.

Rockson gripped the wheel, careening around abandoned cars and debris in the streets. People jumped out of his way. "What's the fastest way to the dump?" he shouted at Kim.

"That way!" said Kim, stabbing a finger at a boulevard to the right. "Slow down! You're driving like a maniac!"

Rockson couldn't help but smile to himself. That was exactly what the real Kim said to him every time he got behind a wheel. He pressed the pedal to the metal, accelerated toward the turn.

"You're going to get us all killed!" Kim yelled as a man leapt out of the taxi's path.

"I always drive like this," Rockson said. "Relax."

"Holy fucking hell!" blurted Kim as the momentum of the turn threw her into Rockson. She clapped a hand to her mouth. She had never uttered an obscenity in her life. It was an indication that the tranquilizers were wearing off. She suddenly felt liberated.

In the back seat, Barbara stared to wail. Within moments, Teddy junior also lost control and began crying. Kim tried to quiet them, to no avail.

Rockson tore through the streets. Fires raged in many of the buildings throughout the chessboard

241

sectors, and people dashed about the streets carrying their booty. Some were trying to put out the fires. Frantic men and women tried to flag him down; if he was escaping this madness, they wanted to hitch along. He steeled his heart against them and sped by.

Scattered gunfire came from the sidewalks. Rockson ducked as a man ran out into the street firing a pistol at them. A bullet cracked a corner of the windshield into a spiderweb. "Get the kids down!" he ordered Kim.

Sobbing, she crawled over the seat and pushed the screaming children to the floor, covering them with her body. She raised her head to peek over the seat. "Turn left up there," she said. "That will take you to the highway."

Rockson downshifted and careened left, shifting up and accelerating as he executed the turn. Another car turned into the street from an opposite corner, and sped up until it was even with Rockson's taxi. He glanced to his left. The car was jammed with Runners, driven by a grinning Barrelman. He gave the thumbs-up sign and hit the gas pedal, pulling ahead.

Other vehicles joined in the escape—cars, trucks, taxis, even motorcycles. Soon a ragtag parade was screaming toward the highway out of town. Some contained Runners; others contained desperate citizens who followed in the hopes that the drivers of the fleeing cars knew something they didn't and were heading for safety.

Not everyone made it, even to the highway. A few drivers lost control at their high speeds, ending in fiery crashes. One car smashed head-on into a telephone pole, pushing the front end into a vee that reached the back seat. A pickup truck took a turn too fast and overturned, crushing the cab in a shower of sparks.

Rockson, at the lead, kept a watch in his rear-view and side mirrors. It pained him greatly to see the wrecks, but there was nothing he could do. He kept his foot on the accelerator.

They reached the highway, an open, empty ribbon of asphalt that stretched away into the shimmering horizon. Rockson pushed the taxi for all it was worth—which wasn't much, in his estimation, even considering the primitive nature of the car. A hundred miles an hour wasn't fast enough. At such high speed, the car vibrated so badly Rockson thought it would shake apart.

He kept an eye on Barrelman's taxi behind him. The leader of the Runners was keeping the second lead position. Behind him stretched the train of racing vehicles that shifted and jockeyed for position.

Barrelman fell further and further behind Rockson—his car simply couldn't keep up the speed. Then Rock heard an explosion and saw the car weave and bounce all over the road, out of control. Two cars coming up fast from behind nearly crashed into it; the drivers did some fancy swerving to avoid a collision.

"Oh, my God," said Kim, looking out the rear window. "A blowout!"

Barrelman's taxi continued to fishtail, then dove off the highway in a cloud of dust, turning over on the sunbaked ground. Somehow it remained intact.

Rockson slowed and yanked the wheel, turning the car off the highway in a wide arc. The tires struck the

243

dirt and the taxi bounced fiercely as Rockson headed back in the opposite direction.

"What are you doing?" Kim yelled.

"Going back for a friend," Rockson said between gritted teeth. Other vehicles shot by on the highway like bullets, sunlight glinting off the metal.

Rockson screeched to a halt by Barrelman's crippled car, which sat lopsided, steam billowing from the radiator. Barrelman and the seven other Runners who were jammed into the car were disentangling themselves and crawling out.

"Shit!" screamed Barrelman, jumping up and down. He kicked the car.

Rock rolled down the window. "Leave it and get in!"

"There's not enough room," said Barrelman, peering into the windows. "Go! Get your family to the Portal!"

"We'll make room." Rockson put the taxi in neutral and pulled the emergency brake. He climbed out and opened the back door. "Double up back here, as many as possible. Put the kids on your laps." He strode to the rear of the car and opened the trunk. "Someone can get in here. We're almost at the dump—there should be enough air. I can take two up front."

The Runners complied, and when everyone was stuffed into the taxi, Rockson got behind the wheel and screamed back onto the highway. The other vehicles were long gone. Within seconds, he was in high gear and pushing the taxi back to top speed. The big engine sounded like a marimba band gone crazy.

Soon the horizon changed. The air had been shimmering but clear; now it shimmered but was increasingly opaque. They were approaching the Veil that surrounded Salt Lake City. And there was the Portal. It had grown larger; it was now the size of a building, and still growing. The spiraling mass of ocher and violet shimmered and danced over the dump.

It looked like the eye of the Devil himself.

The distance to the city dump was deceiving; the mountain of refuse took precious minutes to reach, and then it seemed to burst upon them. Rockson decelerated down the ramp, pulling alongside the cars that had already arrived. The other refugees were standing around or wandering without direction, not knowing what to do next. No one had ever gone through the Portal except for a few of the drunks among them.

Rockson and the others extricated themselves from the car. Those who had never before been to the dump murmured in awe at what they saw. The multicolored swirling Portal struck them silent. It sat directly on mountains of refuse three times as high as a human being. The air around the dump was thick and oppressive, almost palpable; it smelled of ozone as well as of refuse, and crackled with electricity. The world seemed to stop at the dump; nothing was visible through the silver-gray curtain. The Portal beckoned. Mesmeric.

Rockson glanced at the watch on his wrist. Six P.M. Four minutes to zero hour. Four minutes to get into the Portal — and hopefully the time-tunnel that had brought Rockson to this mad place.

He saw a change in the Time-Portal's "Bloody Eye" appearance at the end of the dump. "There's a clear

245

spot in the Portal—it must be the time-tunnel opening up." He grabbed the kids, one in each arm, and took off on a run through the middle of the dump, slipping and sliding over loose heaps of garbage. Behind him clattered Kim, Barrelman, and the mob of refugees. They were convinced now, thank God.

The kids, who had simmered down in the taxi, opened up their lungs again, screaming for Mommy. Everyone was crying and gasping, going down in the greasy rubble and struggling up again. As they came upon the Portal, several Runners lost their courage and turned away, choosing fear of the known rather than fear of the unknown.

Barrelman stopped and screamed at them, begging them to keep going. "Come on! You can't quit now! You'll be killed!"

Rockson twisted and shouted at Barrelman. "Hurry! We've only got seconds!"

With a look of anguish, Barrelman turned and scurried toward Rockson.

A set of long streaks—white vapor trails—appeared high in the darkening sky above, to the north. At first, Rockson thought it was the electricity in the Portal—perhaps the movement of time itself. Then another thought struck him dead in the heart: maybe it was the trails of nuke missiles, launched thousands of miles away and coming down on their targets.

"Faster!" he shouted behind him. "Move it!"

Chapter 19

Rockson didn't know what would happen when they entered the Portal. He worried that they'd just be pushed back by the invisible force. But maybe this time — as the city disappeared in the flash of atomic hellfire — the Portal would take them to 2092 A.D. It was a theory, a hope, a chance. A chance they *had to take*.

With a sharp intake of air and a tight grip on Kim's hand, Rock plunged forward. There was a sickening wrench. A blurry nothingness, red, like looking at the sun through closed eyelids — and then howling wind. Cold. Dark.

Kim and the kids were still with Rockson. So were scattered groups of the Runners — but where was he? There was no ground, no sky. Rockson was slowly rotating, floating in a blue-black darkness punctuated by flashes of brilliant color — as if he were hurtling among strobe lights. No gravity.

Rockson's hand had been wrenched away from Kim, but she was tumbling nearby. He could see her in the flickering colored lights, and he shouted to her:

Kim, I'm here.

He felt his vocal cords move, but heard nothing. No sound. The brilliant flashes moved away, behind him, giving the appearance that he was moving at great velocity upward—though, of course, it must be an illusion.

How much time was passing? It seemed like a few minutes ago at most that they had jumped into the Portal, yet there was no way to tell. Another part of the universe—another dimension—that's where he might be—where *they* might be.

And they might never return to the world they knew.

Then there was a hissing sound, and the blackness disintegrated like a moth-eaten stage curtain. Rockson, still spinning wildly, was out among the stars. There was no sun, just stars. The Milky Way, stretching all around him. The nearest constellations—Orion, Leo, were there. But their stars were incredibly bright, and *moving*. But that was impossible! For the stars themselves to appear to move meant that Rockson was traveling thousands of times faster than light. Impossible. Unless . . . unless he was also traveling in *time* as well as in space. But that wasn't the only thing happening that was impossible. In the vacuum of space, he shouldn't have been able to breathe. His body should have exploded from its internal pressure. Yet he felt fine, and breathed regularly, easily. He just gave up at this point and let it all happen. He relaxed into the trip. Wherever the hell he was going, it sure was beautiful!

A portion of the Milky Way—that hundred-billion-star, disk-shaped group our sun and all its planets belong to—grew brighter in the direction he was heading. Giant blue-white diamondlike stars zipped past him, changing color to red as they passed. The *red shift*. Light itself bending because of intense speed. He'd read of the phenomenon in astronomy textbooks, but had never expected to see the effect personally.

Rock looked around for Kim, the kids, and all the others, but saw no one. He was apparently alone in this silent and beautiful universe. He wasn't afraid, though, for any of them. It was all too spectacular for that.

Now he entered the center of the galaxy itself. It seemed to be sucking him in, along with half the stars in the sky, as it twisted. The galaxy *twisted*. He knew that a galaxy takes billions of years to turn one complete circuit. Yet, in the past minute, he had seen it turn. A billion years had gone by! And what's more, as he fell down, down, down into the black hole in the center of the galaxy, as he fell in with a billion suns as traveling companions, he should have been vaporized by the heat, but he wasn't.

Rockson knew that galaxies come *out* of the black holes in their centers. They don't go *into* them; they spin *out* of the black hole. That means he was traveling backward in time, a billion years per minute.

Where to next? He soon found out. There was a hissing sound, and as his body became a flat rainbow arching through the black hole, as it became a billion-mile-long strand of varying colors, he momentarily lost consciousness.

Then he was out the other side of the black hole, in the way a string would pass through the center of a donut.

He felt himself still intact, still dressed in the white suit. He should have been dead a million times. Maybe *that's it,* he thought — *I am dead.* I'm going through what everyone goes through after they die. The Bardo state, the time between death and re-birth — *My God, what a trip!*

There were odd shapes passing him now, large globes of twisted, writhing lights, some double — the quasars. The fundamental original globs of universe-matter that had existed before the galaxies. He must be back ten or fifteen billion years now. And he was still spinning onward toward a central light, just like all the quasars. He realized he would soon be at the beginning of the universe, at the Big Bang itself. At the moment of creation, at the joining of *the all*!

In just a moment it happened. He, and it, and everything, *was one*. He was all-conscious, all-being, *all-everything.*

Then, with a sickening wrench, *it* exploded outward, *it* became separate things — quasars, galaxies, stars, and, finally, worlds.

And Rockson saw the earth ahead; a blue-and-white globe, hurtling at him like a cannonball.

He entered the atmosphere, expecting to burn up from the speed, and yet he didn't. Rockson seemed to drift, like a leaf, over fields of tall fern trees. He now saw dinosaurs grazing down there. Then he was lower, and suddenly he was not Rockson, but a little shrewlike creature, running around under the feet of the dinosaurs. He was the first mammalian ancestor of man. And then he went through a hundred, a thousand, a million lives, all in the flickering of an

250

eye. He graduated through the classes of larger mammals: a tree-climbing monkey; an apelike creature with a club; a stooped-over, hairy man. And then — he was a human.

After fifteen million lives, he was a human, a struggling nomadic hunter, living with a band of other similar human creatures. And he was frightened, hungry, cold. Finding a caribou, he smashed its brains out, eating the raw meat. He did that for a hundred, a thousand lifetimes. Hunted.

Then there was fire, sacred fire, started by lightning and kept alive by a member of the tribe, who watched over it while the others hunted. And when they returned to their cave, their ate not raw, but cooked meat. And it was good.

Then Rockson was a man stooping over primitive corn plants, tending them, watering them, backbreaking day after backbreaking day.

There were great floods, and earthquakes. He was a priest, a priest of the Pharaoh of ancient Egypt, predicting the time of reincarnation of the Pharaoh, who had just died. The Pharaoh was embalmed. And all the priests, including Rockson — his name was Ta-Ah-Nek at the time — were forced to commit suicide and be buried with the Pharaoh, so that in the time to come the Pharaoh would have company. And the great, absurd vanity that Rockson had possessed in his life as the Pharaoh's priest led to a hundred future lives of humbleness for him, to atone.

Then a hundred more incarnations — lives of desperation in north India, wealth in China, in the Pacific Islands. Lives in times when humans no longer understood their place in the universe, times when they no longer were aware of the fact that a lifetime is an instant, just a building block to another, then another, life.

And mankind became — evil. Murder, war, delusion after delusion came. And the few souls that transcended it all, and out of their compassion *tried* to tell the others *the truth*, were martyred. Crucified. Stoned. Burned at the stake. And man knew not what he was . . .

And slowly, slowly, the karmic progress of his soul occurred. He would not kill, he would not eat human flesh. Then Rockson was a textile worker in early industrial England — toiling twelve hours a day for subsistence wages. Yet he did not hate, he did not lash out in his anger. More karmic progress occurred. His soul rose higher in the chain of evolution. Others fell and rose on the karmic chain, some devolving to animals again because of their lack of compassion. But slowly, slowly, despite pitfalls, the Rockson moved ahead, evolving until . . .

There was a *scream*. And it was Rockson's scream. He had landed on a desert.

He was Ted Rockson, the Doomsday Warrior. A twenty-first-century human being. And after seeing it all, the beginning of everything, after being the Oneness, the evolution of the stars, of the galaxies, of life on earth, after seeing the millions of lifetimes of birth and painful death and rebirth, Rock fell to his knees and wept. He wept for himself, and for all life. He wept for all the ignorant, striving souls lost on the endless wheel of time.

And his fists closed on the sand. The sand grains slipped through his hands, fell to the ground.

He looked around. A deep-blue sky above; the air cold and thin in his lungs; flickering green strontium clouds high in the western sky.

He was back. Back in 2092 A.D.

Back where he belonged. He looked around him, stood up. Yes! There was Kim, and the kids, and Barrelman, standing there, looking like they were frozen in shock.

"Did you see—did you experience all of *that*?" Rock asked Kim, coming up to her and taking her cold left hand. She looked pale, so pale.

"Experience what? The last thing—thing—I—remember is you pulling me into the Portal."

"You didn't see it, see everything?" Rock asked. He gave up trying to explain.

"No. Did something happen? Did we make it?"

Rock sighed. "We made it, Kim. We made it."

There were practical matters to attend to—like getting the group together again before they wandered away in the desert—and keeping an eye out for the Soviets.

It seemed that only Barrelman, of all the Runners who had approached the Portal, had crossed over. That saddened Rock, but there was nothing to be done about it. He hoped the others might have "fallen" someplace or some*time* else safely. He gathered his wife, kids, and friend and started . . .

Soon, Rockson found scattered debris—bits of Soviet clothing, a pistol which he picked up and slipped into his belt. He wished it were the compound gun. A pistol wouldn't do in this age. He headed toward an area filled with debris. It contained the empty missile silo Streltsy had taken him to. Rock found its roof blown off. The time-tornado had done its handiwork here. Dead Russians lay scattered everywhere, some beginning to rot. They were being picked upon by birds.

Days must have passed since he'd left! Startled by his presence, the cloud of buzzards swooped up from the charnel pit that had once been a silo-home for the perverted Soviet officers. He told Kim and the others to wait, then climbed down and took a submachine gun and some clips. How was it that none of these Reds had come into the past with him? Possibly it was because they had no counterpart back in Salt Lake City 1989. That must be it. They had stayed here and gotten smashed to pieces by the tornado. All except Streltsy, of course. He had a counterpart back in 1989 — *Chessman*!

Rockson took the supplies he needed — canteens of water, some Soviet rations in canisters, ammo, and headed southeast, walking in the harsh light of the setting orange sun, with his strangely silent entourage. He could see the snow-capped Rockies in the distance.

They walked onward for about an hour, saw the first stars come out in the flickering green clouds of strontium high above.

Soon, Rock thought, the sky would be a dark place filled with the guiding lights that would direct them home. They stopped to rest. Kim, particularly, was feeling the strain. She didn't look right at all. Neither did the kids, nor Barrelman. Rockson wondered what would happen when he reached Century City with them. After all, Kim had a counterpart in this time-space. The kids didn't — and neither did Barrelman.

The situation was, to say the least, odd.

He passed around the Soviet canteen's water and then Kim stood bolt upright. "Rock, oh, Rock," she wailed, frightened.

"What is it?" He stood too. Were his eyes deceiving him in the dim light of dusk? Kim seemed to be semitransparent.

"Rock. I'm fading away," she shouted. But Kim's shout was just a faint echo. Hollow, fading. Rockson could look through her body. She was becoming like a mist. The kids too, and Barrelman, were fading. They started screaming the same hollow scream. Rockson rushed for Kim, tried to grab her. But his hands went through her body.

"Good-bye . . . Rock . . . good-bye . ." she said. And then she faded away. She was gone. They were all gone.

Rockson stood there alone. He stood there a long, long time, until the night air was so cold that he had to move or freeze to death. He tried to understand. Could it be that they didn't exist? Was it all a dream? Some hallucination brought on by eating the blood-fruit, plus the delirium caused by the torture, by being dragged behind the Soviet jeep?

There was not a *scrap* of evidence to lead him to believe the whole thing—Salt Lake City, the Chessman, the Runners—had ever been real.

But what about his white suit? That was real. He looked down at his body. He was naked. That was why he felt so cold.

If it had *never* happened, if it all had been a dream, the sealskin garment could have been torn from his body by the force of the storm winds. He might never know if Salt Lake City had been a dream—or if *this* was the dream.

Dream or not, it *felt* real enough. He was cold, and he was alone, and he was miles from home. He looked around, found some Soviet garments, in a pile of wind-strewn debris. He put on the best of the lot—a torn field jacket and pair of khakis.

Then he started walking—walking toward home.